Mrs C Remembers

Himanjali Sankar grew up in Kolkata. She studied English Literature at JNU, New Delhi, and taught English at the University of Indianapolis in the US. She has worked with various publishing houses and is currently an editor with Bloomsbury India. Two of her books, *The Stupendous Timetelling Superdog* and *Talking of Muskaan*, were shortlisted for the Crossword Award for Children's Literature. *Mrs C Remembers* is her first novel for adults.

Mrs C Remembers

Himanjali Sankar

PAN

First published in India 2017 by Pan
an imprint of Pan Macmillan India
a division of Macmillan Publishers India Private Limited
Pan Macmillan India, 707, Kailash Building
26 K. G. Marg, New Delhi – 110 001
www.panmacmillan.co.in

Pan Macmillan, The Smithson, 6 Briset Street, London EC1M 5NR,
Basingstoke and Oxford
Associated companies throughout the world
www.panmacmillan.com

ISBN 978-93-86215-15-4

This is a work of fiction. All characters, locations and events are fictitious. Any resemblance to actual events or locales or persons, living or dead, is entirely coincidental.

3

Typeset by SÜRYA
Printed and bound in India by Repro India Ltd

FSC www.fsc.org
MIX
Paper from responsible sources
FSC® C047271

May–July 2002

Mrs Chatterjee

It is not that I have never imagined my mother-in-law's death. The important role I will have to play in all the rituals that follow. Quiet, dignified. I do not want to cry because I have never been the sort of person to cry in public. Even when my own parents passed away – my father ten years back and my mother more recently – I only cried when I was alone in the bathroom. I have never cried in front of my husband either. Only once in front of my daughter but I quickly ran to the bathroom because loss of control is so very humiliating even if in the presence of those one loves most.

My husband does not know how intensely I dislike his mother or all the things she has said or done to me. When I was a newlywed I did try to confide in him once. I tried to do it indirectly as if she had said something funny about my family, not malicious as it really was.

I no longer recollect her reason for ridicule on that occasion. There has been such a steady stream of insults in the course of the last thirty-eight years that it is difficult to remember the exact words, the when and the wherefore. That time it possibly had to do with my father coming from the gutters and my mother marrying him because she was not beautiful enough to find a really good catch from her own socio-economic background.

'But that's true, isn't it?' my husband had said when I told him what his mother had told me. And then and there I decided never to complain about his mother to him or to anyone else for that matter. He is too intelligent to not know if I am complaining even if I couch it in nice words. I appreciate the fact that I am married to a good-looking, intelligent man whom I love with all my heart and who loves me equally well in return. Why should I ruin what we have by bringing his mother into our bedroom?

There were so many restrictions and rules in my in-laws' household that I couldn't help but imagine sometimes how it would be in the future – when I would be free to live the way I wanted. It's not that this was an indecent wish for their early death. Just that after twenty-five or thirty years of marriage, it would be a relief to be able to do as I pleased. To go out without having to first spend an hour with my father-in-law discussing the car and the driver and how long I would be out and where I would go. Not that I minded – being nice to him, just spending a little time with him – discussing his worries and thoughts was an investment that always paid off. My father-in-law was a loving man and devoted to the family. His wife was the problem and he knew that too. He always sided with me which made my mother-in-law very angry, but that was not my fault, was it? If he could recognize his wife for the wicked woman that she was, it had nothing to do with me.

My father-in-law gave me so much that it almost made up for his wife's needless cruelty. Strangely enough, after he passed away, she quietened down even though the bond they had shared was tenuous at best. Quietened down in comparison to what she used to be like. Her tongue remained vicious and slicing but the temper tantrums were few and far between. She never really stopped troubling me till the day she died.

She was practically bedridden and frail for the last three years of her life and completely at my mercy. Her son loved her but didn't spend any time with her. He was immersed in his legal work as men should be. Just peeping into her room on his way to and back from work. He left the caregiving to me. To be honest, all I needed to do was employ nurses to look after her round the clock. Money has never been a concern.

I had to change nurses at least ten times in the last three years which is not surprising. All of them departed in tears. My mother-in-law would use foul language, abuse and torture them in ways that only she is capable of devising. Peeing and shitting on the bed instead of asking for the bedpan. Throwing her food on the ground.

I did not say a word to my husband. Just called the agency and asked for a new nurse and, in the interim,

I doled out huge sums of money to the domestic help so they would take care of her. I entered her room once or twice a day to speak to the nurses, ignored her as far as possible and left.

'Anita, Anita,' she would shout from the bed in her surprisingly loud voice whenever she knew I was outside her room. There was nothing I could do to stop the filthy abuses that usually accompanied her cries, but I would often pretend not to hear. She had no power over me any more.

Only once in the last three years has she managed to truly unsettle me. I was in my bedroom in the afternoon, just recently, resting and reading the newspaper. The curtains were drawn, the bedroom door was shut. Murders, rapes, looting in Gujarat. Muslims were being massacred. When I mention it to my husband he says that the Godhra train burning has to be avenged by the Hindus. Not that he believes in any religious rubbish. But Gujarat has a chief minister who doesn't suck up to the minorities like the Congress clowns. It was all right to sometimes show the minorities who was boss. My husband knows about these things. He particularly likes to make fun of the Congress – my father was a member of the party – without meaning any harm, of course.

So, I am reading all these horrific reports of atrocities when my door is suddenly flung open and she is standing there, her skin hanging in wrinkled folds from her face and arms, her matchstick legs and fat upper body lending her a grotesque appearance. I don't know why the nurse wasn't with her, and how she was walking at all.

'Bitch,' she said in a low whisper. The effort of walking to my room had robbed her voice of its strength. 'Whore. My son slaves day in and day out so you can wear your fancy saris and go out where and when you please. Lolling on the bed without a care in the world. But there is a God up there and he is watching.'

I could not move or get up. It was not that I was unused to the language. Just that she was supposed to be bedridden and my guard wasn't up like it used to be. But that was the last time she ever took me by surprise. I made sure of that. In my own way.

I tried to return to the newspaper after she left. I read the reports of killings and carnage but I could not muster the energy to be horrified any more; they were just words strung together on a page that no longer made sense.

My mother-in-law's face kept floating in front of me as I drifted off into an uneasy sleep. I dreamed she was wielding a trishul, blood dripping from it, a red tika slashed on her forehead and her wispy grey hair, oily and thin, open and flowing. Her widow-white sari and the wrinkled, loose folds of skin under her forearms shook and quivered as she dug the trishul into the pregnant belly of a girl in a salwar kameez who folded her arms and begged for mercy, but my mother-in-law, her eyes bloodshot and venomous, continued to stab her stomach with the trishul like it was a slab of meat. I could not see the girl's face; the veil covering her head was drawn over her face too, right down to her chin.

It felt like I woke up without even falling asleep. I should stop reading the newspapers and magazines that sensationalize just about everything that happens in the country. They are seeping into my dreams, twisting and turning them, till I was nervous and scared. As my husband says, I don't have a proper understanding of these things. He may be right – the walls of my life are opaque, the windows narrow and shut, the air mundane, stale. I don't stride around in wide open spaces, learning and understanding the world in new ways. Anyway, let that be, each to his own and I am happy in my life.

In the evening when he came home, I did not tell him how his bedridden mother had suddenly materialized in our bedroom. But that night I forgot to give her the medicines she was supposed to take. Not forgot so much as postponed till I forgot. The medicines were kept in a small carved mahogany cabinet by her bedside. I couldn't bear the thought of going into her room and taking out the medicines from the drawer while she lay inert on the bed, staring at me fixedly, muttering curses under her breath. Not that the nurses couldn't do it themselves, but I usually handed the medicines to the nurse on duty when I was at home so I knew when the stock was running out. When I was out or busy with something else, I left them instructions. It showed them that I was in control. But that night I didn't leave any instructions.

Both the nurses must've thought the other one had given the medicines.

I started getting careless about Ma's medication after that. Not deliberately, but it was also true that the quality of life she had now was worthless. She deserved to go. It was unfair and selfish of us to pin her to this life through artificial means. In a month's time her condition had deteriorated. She had to be fed through pipes, a fibrous yellowing vegetable receiving meagre nourishment from thin translucent tubes. She could barely whisper any more, let alone shout. Her son started sitting by her side for ten minutes every evening, after returning from court and before his first clients arrived. She stared at him with large, sorrowful eyes, pipes running all over her face and body. He stroked her scant hair and wrinkled arms and her eyes softened. I think I forgave her then.

Sohini

Trust Thamma to die in a way that her funeral should land on the one day that I'd been looking forward to for the last three months. I'm going to have my first exhibition. Not solo, but five of my pieces are going to be displayed and I am hoping at least one of them will find a buyer while I'm in Kolkata for Thamma's shraadh. Even my blouse has been tailored for the launch. Don't think I should wear it for the shraadh – it's backless and revealing.

I loved Thamma – much more than Ma will ever realize. Thamma's tactics were often underhand while Ma didn't really have a strategy to speak of.

'Will you be wearing blouses like your mother when you grow up?' Thamma posed this trick question to me when I must have been nine or ten. 'Cut so low at the back.'

'No, I won't,' I said, uncomfortable but eager to give the right answer. I asked Ma later why her sari blouses were cut that way, revealing so much flesh.

'Are they?' she asked, not really paying attention. 'I like the air to circulate; it's quite hot these days.'

Thamma was a horrid person, I'll grant Ma that. But so very witty and sparkling and sarcastic. Ma could never have won a verbal battle even if she'd tried. Which she didn't. She would sit there looking blank and stoned which wasn't a bad strategy. Thamma would just give up. Mutter something about her daughter-in-law being an idiot and stomp away.

Omar offered to come to Kolkata for Thamma's shraadh with me.

'To hold your hand, Sohini, and just be there with you,' he said. I visualized Omar and myself standing in one corner of our terrace holding hands while the relatives milled around.

'No,' I said. 'I don't need you in Kolkata. To hold my hand or anything else for that matter.'

'Stop with the dirty,' he said. 'Your grandmother is still warm in her grave.'

'My grandmother was the dirtiest woman alive, and dirtiest amongst the dead too, I'm sure. The gaalis she knew, you would've been impressed,' I said. 'Besides, Omar, we don't bury our dead, we burn them.'

'Hai Allah, really?' Omar said, striking his forehead with his palm.

'We Hindus don't like grave metaphors; we can't identify with them,' I persisted.

'Okay, shut up. You want me to come with you or not?' Omar asked.

'No,' I said. Omar has been to Kolkata with me before. But then he only met the family. Not the hordes of relatives who will be descending for the funeral. I don't think my parents would appreciate his presence at the shraadh. The hordes would love it. It would give them something to discuss for the next two and a half years or so.

Omar shrugged and didn't ask again. That's what I love best about him. He never gets offended. I've always thought guys with ponytails don't get offended easily. They are the definition of cool.

On the flight I think of Thamma. Not too many people liked her. Her in-laws disliked her with a vengeance – from her grandmother-in-law to the youngest children of that household – their shared hatred of Thamma kept that branch of our family united. But I do believe she loved my grandfather even though he was intellectually so very inferior to her. She loved him for his looks and because he was her husband. They were programmed like that in the early twentieth century. He didn't love her though. And in return she hated every member of his family – his mom, sisters, aunts, nephews, nieces. She was vicious and mean to each of them, uniformly, impartially. Thakurda could never get a handle on her – he didn't even realize that it was his love that she ultimately wanted, and the meanness and arrogance was a way to cope. He felt humiliated and small around her and, in return, he loved my mother. She was sweet and nice, the perfect daughter-in-law.

Ma was programmed to serve. I don't mean that in a bad way. She's a wonderful person, one of the very best. She can give up her life for me and Sudeep, my brother. She is kind, and loved by everyone who knows her. I have never wanted to have kids, but even if I did I would never be as good a mother as the one I have. She's my rock.

Ma was waiting for me at the airport.

'You didn't have to come; you must be tired,' I said. We didn't hug. It's not something we do in our family. We just start talking as if we last met a couple of hours back. That's our style and I don't mind. It's a confident love that needs no props.

'I expected Thamma to live some more, somehow … even though she was so unwell,' I said.

'Why?' asked Ma, rather sharply.

'Jesus, she's dead. Can't you let it go?' I said.

'It's not that …' Ma tapered off. 'Nothing.'

I shrugged – the signature Omar shrug that I like to imitate. Ma has always been weird about Thamma. I guess if your life till sixty has been defined by this crazy old bat then you can't be very sane yourself. Poor Ma. I handed my suitcase to our driver, Kaloo, who dumped it in the boot. He didn't greet me cheerily as usual, just asked if I was tired after the flight. With downcast eyes and a nod that befitted a pre-funeral conversation. We settled into the car for the long drive home, as Ma told me about the arrangements for the funeral.

'Sudeep and Malini are doing everything – looking after the guest list, menu …' Ma never takes anyone for granted and she feels grateful very easily.

'How's Baba?' I asked.

'He's all right, busy. Today he has gone to meet ... the lady who is going to sing the kirtan. What's her name ... she's very famous, charges a lot ...'

After I first left Calcutta and would go home for the holidays, the journey from the airport to our house would be intense and fraught with memories of the only childhood I would ever know. I was young enough for nostalgia that was fresh and moving and taut with longing. Now I tiredly tried to dredge up that old nostalgia for Calcutta as I stared out of the car window.

'What's happening, happened, in Gujarat ...' Ma began when we had run out of funeral conversation.

'State-sponsored terrorism.' I knew she would neither agree nor quite understand what I meant.

'I dreamt that your Thamma was killing a pregnant Muslim girl, about a month before she died,' Ma continued, ignoring my comment.

'That's horrid. Even for Thamma that's pretty dire,' I said. 'Never mind. Dreams can be merciless.'

'Your Baba thinks the Muslims are getting what they deserve, and I suppose ...' Ma stopped mid-sentence, collected herself, and asked, 'How's Omar?'

I had to laugh. 'He's fine, Ma. He's good.'

'Does he have relatives in Gujarat?' she asked.

'No, Ma, all Muslims don't have relatives in Gujarat or in Egypt or Afghanistan. They could have relatives anywhere, like the rest of us,' I said.

Ma didn't like it when I was sarcastic. 'We do have relatives primarily in Kolkata.' She sounded prim.

'So, Omar has relatives primarily in UP which is where he is from, as you know. Okay?' I wasn't sure if the logic worked but Ma fell silent. I didn't want to tell her about Imran Javed who was Omar's dad's friend. He used to live in a Muslim neighbourhood in Ahmedabad and he was burnt alive in February this year by a violent mob. Even if I did mention it, Ma would possibly just say, see, I was right to ask if Omar has relatives in Gujarat. She can be strangely insensitive for a woman who is quite caring when it comes to the people she loves.

Omar didn't speak a word the whole day on which Imran Javed was burnt alive. His dad told him about it on the phone and he repeated it to me mechanically and then clamped up. I didn't try to make him talk. He mostly sat in front of the TV, and when I nestled up to him, he held me so tight that my ribs hurt. And that night he slept holding me in a way that made it impossible for me to fall asleep for a long time, but I didn't push him away like I would've on any other night.

'Are you thinking of marriage?' Ma asked now. She had moved on from the relatives-in-Gujarat question. Since I'm thirty-five and a divorcee, even a Muslim will do. Besides, Omar's family is wealthy and elite and full of nawabs and begums. Bengalis love the feudal rich; it's got something to do with being British ass-lickers under the Raj.

'No, I'm not thinking of marriage,' I said. 'Though I'm completely happy with Omar, don't worry.'

'But unless you get married you can never be sure,' Ma said.

'Of what?' I asked.

'You know, security, children, family,' she said vaguely.

'I don't want children and I'm secure enough in this relationship with or without marriage. I don't need a marriage certificate to tie Omar to me. It wouldn't make any difference.' This was the first time we were talking about marriage. After I got divorced seven years back, that is.

Ma shook her head, unconvinced.

The apartment Omar and I live in belongs to me. Or to Baba really. Omar is a designer and the rooms are overflowing with typical Omar-ish furnishings – a lamp made from scrap here, a decoupage coffee table there, stools with twisted legs that he assembled with wood he had left over after a project. Omar insists on paying all the bills in lieu of rent and, though I protested at first, it has been useful. It made it possible for me to leave my desk job and concentrate on my art. Fingers crossed, at least one or two of my paintings sell at the exhibition.

'Your Thamma would never have allowed you to marry a Muslim,' Ma said.

'You underestimate her. And now I see why we are suddenly talking about marriage,' I said.

'She always underestimated *me* but I knew her for what she was. Totally,' Ma said.

This was true. Thamma assumed that a person who didn't shout and fight was a wimp. Ma is far from a wimp. She has her own resources and ways of dealing with situations. I think Ma would've flourished in a business school – she has method, diligence and determination, plus a very practical, no-nonsense approach to life. She does manage a huge household with twenty servants. I've seen her ticking off long lists and settling accounts with the servants, planning our investments with her CA, organizing huge parties on the front lawn. All this without ever appearing flustered.

'Ma, you won't miss Thamma at all, will you?' I asked.

'No,' she said. She didn't have any trouble being honest with me. If anyone else had asked she would have muttered platitudes about the house being empty or some such thing. I remember how Ma wasn't at all affected by Thakurda's death and how it had surprised me because she really had been attached to him, or so I had thought. But why would she care about Thamma at all? If anything, she would be relieved.

'Are you relieved she is gone? Were you looking forward to her death?' I asked now.

Ma's face suddenly closed up, like a window shutting on the outside world. I'd pushed it too far.

'Looking forward to her death? Is that what people will think?' Ma asked. So she hadn't minded the question so much as wondered whether it was a socially foregone conclusion – Ma was dreadfully image-conscious, as if people were waiting to tear her down. Like Princess Diana or some other celebrity with a double life. But unlike Diana, she wasn't going to crack and collapse and take a lover or two.

'I don't see how this concerns anyone else. So long as you are fine with what you did,' I said.

'What I did? What did I do?' Ma's voice was shrill. I was taken aback. Five minutes back I was admiring the way she was always calm and collected. It was unsettling to see her so jittery. She is possibly more affected by Thamma's death than she realizes. It's been a long day and I'm not sure how – Stockholm syndrome, maybe.

'Not did, really. Just so long as you are okay with the relationship you had with her. You don't have to justify anything to anyone.' I was too surprised by her tone and was rambling.

'Why should I have to justify anything at all? I know what I put up with all my life. I won't say this to anyone except you and Sudeep, but the fact remains the woman was evil and she put me through hell and back.'

I wasn't enjoying this conversation. I don't believe in social niceties, but this was a little indecent – Ma's urge to emphasize how horrid Thamma had been just days after her death.

I suppose she must be tired of faking sorrow with the friends and relatives. Kolkata society is the most hypocritical ever. Narrow minds, paucity of thoughts. I've been through a divorce in this city and am amply qualified to say this – the crocodile tears of relatives who just want gossip, the eager phone calls from grand-aunts who one last spoke to years ago. Or perhaps that's the signature of relatives the world over. Though there is a balance, the small set who compensate, the ones who genuinely care and make you realize no one else really matters.

We were nearly home. Thank god. I leaned forward to catch the first glimpse of the house. I always do that. I spot the windows of the first floor, open wide, and the roof which is tiled with red. I notice the creepers climbing haphazardly all over the walls. It really is a beautiful house and, once again, I felt a rush of pleasure just looking at it, despite Ma's strange mood, despite Thamma not being there to greet me. Not this time and not ever again.

Mrs Chatterjee

I wonder why Sohini said she had expected her Thamma to live some more. She had been dying for three long years. We should all be happy that she led a full life (even if, truth be told, at the expense of other people's happiness). The doctor came to the house at least five or six times in the last one month as her condition was deteriorating. He changed the dosages of some medicines and explained the new medication to me. It was all very confusing, but I took care of things to the best of my abilities. I was so tired the last one month.

'Mrs C, you look quite unwell yourself,' Dr Banerjee had said with concern. He was young and handsome and called me Mrs C which Sohini would tease me about.

'I'm fine, I'm fine,' I told him.

'You're sure the nurses are administering the medicines properly?' he asked me, frowning.

'We have a new nurse. The old one had to suddenly leave,' I explained. This was nothing new in our household as Dr Banerjee himself knew. Though the last one month, Ma had been too unwell to really trouble the nurses. I sacked this one because she was getting nosey and interfering. Went as far as to ask me one day if I was giving Ma the correct doses and even offered to take over in case it was too confusing for me. I let her take over since she was such a know-all. But two days later I asked her to leave as one of the earlier nurses had offered to come back – she was out of work and elderly and poor; it was just that earlier Ma had driven her up the wall. The poor lady hadn't wanted to leave, she was really very needy.

'Senile, incompetent witch,' Ma had said through gritted teeth. 'You will obviously want her to look after me.'

'It's up to you. She doesn't talk too much. Works well. Listens to instructions,' I had replied.

'Your instructions because that is what you've taught her,' Ma said. 'Never mind that it is my son who pays for her.'

'I will ask the agency for a substitute if that's what you want,' I said, ignoring her remarks like I always did. I knew when it was best to give in. No point waiting for her to throw temper tantrums and abuse the poor nurse till she left.

Now that Ma was in no condition to drive anyone up the wall any more, I asked the poor lady to come back. She was hardly a senile, incompetent witch – just tired and listless. I only let the interfering one go when the previous one confirmed she could return. I gave her extra money and told her flatteringly that she'd get a new position anywhere as she was so efficient while the old one who was returning was so needy.

It is strange how life teaches us to be devious. I was always a good person. I have done my best to serve well those closest to me which includes my mother-in-law. Baba was devoted to me; if I wanted I could have tattled to him about Ma but I did not. I used Baba's love to get things done for the family instead: permission for Sohini to study abroad, for Sudeep to play football which Baba felt was a waste of time. When it came to getting something done for Sudeep, it was easy; he was the centre of Baba's life from the day he was born. He couldn't say no to anything Sudeep wanted while Sohini would have to work twice as hard. I did not enjoy that as a mother, watching Sohini fight for something her brother was granted just by virtue of being male.

Baba was generally a sweet person. It wasn't his fault that he belonged to an age when only boys mattered. He took pride in Sohini in his own way. Sohini was always a star student in school. I once heard Baba reciting her marks to our relatives. I suppose my mind has always been clouded by how traumatized everyone was (especially my father-in-law) when she was born.

Baba gave me a lot. He was proud of the fact that I was a graduate in Mathematics with a first-class degree – the first woman in their family to hold such credentials, and in Mathematics no less. He would boast to anyone who would listen that I could drive a car, play tennis and speak in English like a white person. It was embarrassing but I felt loved. The women in my husband's family were really very backward. It was not that anyone forced them to not go to college but they did not care about structured learning. Some of them were quite talented but they did not have discipline. It was not that the men would have said no if they had wanted to study further but they did not bother.

I don't get this feminism-sheminism that Sohini goes on about. You do what you want and let the men do what they want. Live and let live, I will say. But Sohini gets angry with me.

'Don't you understand? It's conditioning that makes women want what they want. It's not a choice as much a result of the stereotypes we grow up with,' she will usually say things like that.

'And only you know how to think properly. I suppose the rest of us women are fools,' I try to joke with her but she gets even more angry. I have brought her up too honestly. I don't regret it at all but I can see that it is part of the problem.

'Men are superior ... it is something we have to accept,' I told her when she was growing up. 'You should not feel bad because your brother is given preference over you by your grandfather. It is only because you are a girl.'

As a child she did not have a problem with that logic. I told her that people who said otherwise were hypocrites. Whatever it may be, no one really thinks of men and women as equals. They just pretend to, so that they can appear modern. And, anyway, what is wrong with the life women lead? Stay at home like queens while the men slave and earn.

The only time I have seen my father-in-law seriously disappointed with me was when Sohini was born. I had been hoping and praying for a boy because I knew how important it was for my husband's family. From the time I was pregnant everyone called the foetus 'he'. When Sohini was born and the nurse told my father-in-law it was a girl he was dreadfully upset. Hoping against hope, he unwrapped the sheet that the newborn baby was wrapped in to check her genitals. He just left the hospital after that, without even looking at me once.

My husband wasn't angry with me though. He knew it was not my fault. He said it was okay and we could have one more child later. He did not say what would happen if that was a girl too. When I went home with the baby I touched my father-in-law's feet and he took a quick look at the baby.

He grimaced and said, 'She's dark. It will be difficult to find a groom for her.' But at least he acknowledged her presence in our lives with that statement. My mother-in-law was secretly delighted that I had failed to give birth to a son. Even though it was her own grandchild. She was happy to find me out of favour with her husband. I knew her well enough by then to understand that. She cursed me in front of my father-in-law that day when I touched her feet. And Baba pretended not to hear. Earlier he would have shouted at her for being mean to me.

My husband did not say anything to support me in front of his mother either as we stood there with our three-day-old daughter. But that night he stroked my hair and my cheek and told me not to worry, that everything was going to be all right. I fell in love with him once again when he spoke like that, so gently, with understanding.

Sohini was a sullen baby, at least at home. No one cared for her and she knew it. No one but me, that is. I know I overcompensated by going out of my way for her. I still feel overprotective towards her. My husband feels I am to blame for the way she is. Me and my parental family. They always favoured Sohini over Sudeep. She was the first grandchild in the family after all.

My husband once said that she wouldn't be a divorcee if I'd brought her up better. But he did not mean it. He is proud of her too, as he should be. She really is an intelligent and good girl.

It was at Presidency College where these destructive ideas entered her head. Impractical ideas, but I could see their appeal. She would come home and share all her newly learnt ideas, and I have to admit, they made sense in some ways. Ideas of social-economic justice, Nehru–Gandhi–Ambedkar, the welfare state and so many other concepts and political matters. She insisted on coming back from college by bus while the car and driver waited at home, something I found rather ridiculous. My father-in-law said girls in our family don't travel by bus. Sohini said nothing to him, but the next day she took the bus home and the poor driver came home two hours later after waiting at College Street and watching the last student leave.

The amount of covering up I had to do for Sohini was tiring. To her credit, she never talked back to her grandparents or father. Silently nodded but did exactly what she wanted to. But I had to listen to her grievances and try to calm her down as well as I could.

My sister used to talk like Sohini – she still does – that is why they are so close. Sanchita is eight years younger than me and we have always been very different from each other. When I was going to get married she turned up her nose and said, 'The family seems rather conservative; are you going to be all right there?'

'We have chosen a handsome, very educated man to be her husband. Why won't she be all right?' I remember Ma feeling really annoyed with Sanchita. I was irritated too. Sanchita was fourteen years old then. What did she know about marriage and such affairs? But my father was always indulgent towards her.

'We will find a different sort of family for you,' he had said to her, smiling. 'Modern, smart.'

It upset me to hear that. My own father didn't think my husband was modern and smart? Though I knew my husband's family members were conservative, now that I was going to be a part of that family, I did not like to hear them being criticized. Sanchita wasn't pacified by Baba's comments either. He needlessly pampered her, which she of course didn't recognize or appreciate.

'That makes me sound like cattle – sell me off to the smartest bidder,' Sanchita said. As far as our father was concerned, she could get away with murder, but Ma couldn't take her backchat.

'What sort of talk is that?' she said sharply. 'Your sister is getting married into one of the most renowned families in Calcutta. If they heard the sort of things you say they would cancel the wedding. And I would not blame them.'

'Will zip my mouth in front of them. Don't worry, Ma,' she said and walked away without a care in the world.

Which is what she really did. Hardly spoke to any of my in-laws, looked bored in their company and made very little effort with my husband too. He tried to get to know her in the beginning. We took her with us to the movies, and for dinner to Sky Room, but Sanchita always appeared reserved and was quick to judge every casual comment he made. And I know I cannot blame him for that. But Sanchita and Sohini were very close from the beginning. It was always Mashi this and Mashi that and, Sanchita, who as a sister had always been uncaring, was a different person when it came to being a mashi. This much I will acknowledge. Even after she had her two boys, she continued to look after Sohini like she was her first-born.

The only time that my father and Sanchita didn't agree with each other was during the Naxal movement of the late 1960s and early '70s. I was busy with my in-laws, my husband and small children in those days and, in any case, I'd never been a very political person, unlike Baba and my sister. One time I remember visiting my parents' home in the middle of the day because I had half an hour to kill before a doctor's appointment. I was walking down the corridor leading to the dining room when I heard raised voices.

'It's dangerous, shona, students are getting killed every day. Please don't …' my father was pleading.

'How can you say that, Baba? You don't really believe that. You never taught me that a person should only protect their own narrow self-interests …' Sanchita stopped talking as I entered the room and the look that Baba and she exchanged in that moment made me feel excluded from the family I was born into. I was a stranger. They did not want to argue in front of me.

'The model daughter-in-law and wife is here,' said Sanchita. 'The exploitation of the working classes must continue, says my sister's father-in-law, and my sister nods in agreement.'

'My father-in-law said no such thing,' I said. Her words stung. She always needled me about my in-laws with comments which made no sense. 'I don't understand what you are saying, Sanchita.'

'You wouldn't,' she said. 'Where are Sohini and Sudeep? I have something for them.'

I let it go. What else could I do? She was my only sister. In the early 1970s, my husband worked very hard. He was slowly getting recognition in his line of work. We were invited to many fancy parties. I would often leave Sudeep and Sohini with my sister at night. She loved having them. I know she has Sohini's best interests at heart, but from a young age Sohini has been too influenced by Sanchita. I don't think she would have been so messed up in her twenties if it hadn't been for Sanchita and the way she taught her to be aggressive and selfish.

Even though Sohini came for only three days this time for her Thamma's shraadh, she had to go over and meet her Mashi.

'You met her at the shraadh,' said her father. Over the years his relationship with my sister hasn't quite improved.

'Not enough,' said Sohini, though she knew her father wouldn't like that. Sudeep does not make an effort to keep up with relatives. Since he lives in Calcutta he is forced to meet them now and then which he feels is enough. His wife is not a Bengali and doesn't understand our customs too well but she is a good girl. She is well-educated too. She has good features, though she is rather dark-skinned as people from her part of the country often are.

My grandson Sumeet is three years old. At the shraadh he wore the kurta pyjama that I had got for him. All the relatives kept pinching his cheeks and hugging and kissing him. He did not mind at all; he smiled and spoke so charmingly that I felt he would grow up to be a famous statesman or politician like my father. Poor boy. He loves being around family. But Malini makes sure he stays busy with so many activities and classes that he never has time to rest or just be with his grandparents.

I've told Sudeep and Malini that a child needs a mother at home when he is small, but it is their decision. Malini works like a man, going to office every day. My son earns enough money for both of them, but Sohini tells me it is not always about money. Sohini is fond of her sister-in-law and very attached to her nephew.

'Come on, Ma. She has a demanding job.' Sohini sounded so impatient. 'You are here for Sumeet – you love your grandson – why do you want Malini to sit at home too?'

I didn't want to needlessly argue so I let it go. I do wish Sohini would get married. It took me a little time to get used to the idea of a boy from a different religion. Malini, after all, is a Hindu, a Brahmin really. But Omar comes from a very wealthy and famous background in Lucknow. My husband knows the family – very cultured, which is so important. Omar is a nice boy, too, so refined and good-looking, and from Cambridge. I am not sure why he keeps a ponytail. I told Sohini she should ask him to get a normal haircut.

'You could just drop a hint, he would listen to you,' I said. 'You know the way we women always do, nicely, without hurting anyone's feelings.'

'You're so funny, Ma,' Sohini said, laughing. 'I love his hair. I don't want him to cut it.'

Omar asked me the very next day if I didn't like his ponytail. He asked in a light-hearted way but I was so embarrassed. Sohini lacks tact; she doesn't know what should or should not be shared with a partner.

'Just not used to the idea, you know. Of boys having long hair. But Sohini says she likes it,' I said to him.

'I was actually planning to chop my hair off when I first met Sohini, but she wouldn't let me,' said Omar. 'Why don't you convince her that I would look better with short hair?'

I think he was teasing me, being playful. So I joked back, 'Sohini has never listened to me. She's impossible!'

It would give me great happiness to see Sohini settle down before I get any older. I know she says no children, but women nowadays have babies at forty even – it's not too late for her.

'It's not a question of too late. I don't feel the need. Besides, I have my Sumeet, don't I?' Sohini says. She's devoted to her nephew. She'll make such a good mother – better than Malini who is, truth be told, a little cold and mechanical. It's because she works so hard, always in the laboratory. If you spend all day examining blood cells and tissues, how will you learn to enjoy life and relax with your husband and child?

Sohini

'Do you feel there's something wrong with Ma? Something a little off?' I asked Sudeep when the last guests had left and it was just him, Malini and me, and an exhausted Sumeet asleep with his head on my lap. Ma and Baba were in their bedroom.

'Not really. Thamma just passed away; Ma will need a bit of time getting used to that,' said Sudeep.

'Her arch-nemesis passed away after a nearly forty-year-long battle. So yes, she's naturally feeling a little bereft, but I don't mean that,' I said. Malini giggled. She and I get along quite well. While Ma just pretends to like her.

'Then what?' Sudeep wasn't really interested but asked politely.

'So, when I got off the aeroplane I expected to see her doing cartwheels on the tarmac, but no,' I said and Malini giggled again. 'She was in a strange zone somehow. All edgy, brittle and angry.'

'I suppose it affected her in ways she didn't expect. It happens in the face of death,' Malini said, and she might've been right.

'How did your art exhibition go?' Sudeep asked before I could say anything more about Ma. He doesn't like talking about parents, emotions and things like that. Probably thinks it's indecent and ungrateful to do so. Come to think of it, we hardly talk to each other. But I love being with him. It just makes me feel secure and warm to be around my little brother who used to be known as Sohini's little lamb, following me everywhere, when he was small.

'According to Omar, fabulously well. Though from the sound of it, I would say averagely well. Two of my pieces got sold at a fairly decent price. And the exhibition got pretty good publicity too,' I said.

'Such a pity you missed it,' said Malini and I nodded. Omar said on the phone that all the women were hitting on him because he looked so dashing in his kurta pyjama and stole. Some men, too, he said.

'I get it. Mankind in general finds you irresistible,' I told him. 'Tell me more about the exhibition. We can discuss your charms later.'

'My magnificent depravity. Aneesh was there too and he said he would definitely write about your work. He thinks you are brilliant, by the way,' Omar said.

'He does?' I was pleased and flattered. Aneesh is an art critic and friend. I wouldn't expect favours from him and nor would he dole out any.

'What was ... your art about? As in, what did you use?' Sudeep was now asking. He wasn't doing a great job faking interest but I was dying to talk about it so didn't mind.

'All sorts of stuff – oils, of course, but also charcoal and collage with old newspapers and garbage,' I said. Sudeep tried not to look horrified. Garbage didn't sound good, I will admit. 'I didn't rummage in the trash cans or anything. Just old stuff that was lying around.'

Sudeep looked vaguely relieved, Malini looked quite interested. For a person who does serious, useful research in a laboratory day in and day out, she is a fun-loving person. A little shy because scientists lack social skills – that's the stereotype and I do feel it's fairly accurate. But behind Malini's thick, unfashionable spectacles lies a happy pair of slightly unsocial eyes.

I had a sudden fit of longing for Omar. There is a must-remember-to-tell-Omar diary in my head and, when it starts filling up, I die to be with him. Always happens when we are apart for a few days.

I want to tell him how odd my family is, yet how normal. How Baba and Sudeep only ever discuss politics and work. How Ma potters around trying to make sure everyone is comfortable and peaceful. She loves peace, as we all do. Which is why we never have arguments or shout and scream.

I love being with my family for a few weeks in a year. After my divorce, I stayed at home for three months. We never discussed why I was there, and everyone was nice but jittery around me. I was miserable; told Baba I had to move out and he suggested I go to Delhi, find a job and stay in his apartment there. Best decision of your life, Omar says, your dad's a dude, and I have to say I agree. About the best decision part. Dad's not a dude unless dude implies only maleness which he qualifies for by default. I had really wanted to move to New York since I'd done my art diploma there but Baba and Ma were keen I didn't go so far away, and in retrospect I'm glad I didn't.

Sumeet was waking up. I ruffled his hair. His cheeks were flushed and criss-crossed with the design of my sari. How much I love this child, yet can't imagine having one of my own. According to Omar, that's because I don't want to clean a newborn baby's poop.

'I think I'm going to steal you when you are five. He will be potty-trained by then, won't he?' I asked Malini.

'I do potty in the bathroom,' Sumeet said proudly.

'Then I can steal you already,' I told him. 'Can you stay without Amma and Baba?'

'Not in the night.'

'Okay, so I will send you home every evening. Can you go home alone in an aeroplane every evening?'

Sumeet shook his head.

'I will wait till you are five in that case,' I said.

'Okay,' he said, looking a little relieved. 'I will sleep with Thammi tonight.'

My parents are devoted to Sumeet. My mother's affections have always been linear and conventional – she loves those she is supposed to love. When it comes to Sudeep and me, her love is fierce and primal. She struggles to love Baba's family and Malini, but doesn't quite manage it. Baba she loves like a prized possession. He is the feather in her cap. Her Empress of Blandings, if I may. A manly man, successful, good-looking. She likes manliness in men – once when I told her that Omar was depressed and unhappy about a project he was working on, she asked me how I knew that.

'Because he tells me about it?' I said.

'Your dad hasn't ever told me about his work troubles,' she said proudly. 'Once I got to know at a party, from his colleagues, what a tough patch he had been through but he'd never told me a thing about it. He never troubled me or made me anxious in any way.'

'How wonderfully stoic,' I said. 'His mother did all the troubling then. Whole family's share.'

'That's got nothing to do with him.' Ma sounded annoyed. She does worship the ground Baba treads on. Or she tries to. She believes it's her duty to fawn on him. She has a mildly superior air when she talks about other people's husbands.

'Sudha's husband told her to take a taxi to the club,' I remember her saying while I was still in college, towards the end of the first year. I remember this particular argument because it was the first of many. I think it was the first time I was seeing my mother the way an outsider might, a person who didn't lead a life like ours.

'And?' I asked. The taxi driver must have tried to molest her was my immediate conclusion. Class baggage is tough to jettison!

'Nothing. But he could've sent the car and driver for her,' Ma said. 'Your Baba would never ask me to take a taxi.'

I'd grown up hearing Ma say such things. But the fact that such a comment was fraught with centuries of chauvinism struck me breathless for the first time. Smack in the face and I was suddenly very angry.

'So your husband cares for you more than hers does for her? Is that what you are saying?' I asked.

'The women in this family don't take public transport. It's just not decorous,' she said.

'I do.'

'Because you don't listen.' And there was a note of pride in her voice when she said that. It's impossible to know what Ma actually believes or thinks. She is blind and unquestioning when it comes to Baba, Sudeep and me. Even when we don't agree with each other, she agrees with all of us! She's not intellectually deficient so much as extremely flexible. It's her mechanism for coping. If you refuse to acknowledge a contradiction or discord it can't exist.

I'm out of here tomorrow. Apart from my mashi, everyone else in Calcutta confuses me. Mashi is kickass. The paradox of my life is that the two women I love the most, my mother and her sister, are always at war. It must have been psychologically damaging for me as a child.

But seriously, I love hearing Mashi's stories of the Naxal movement – she even hid under a bed in a comrade's house during a police search one time. My grandfather packed her off to England when he realized how deeply involved she was in the movement. She hated him for it then but couldn't hold on to her anger for very long. They were very thick, my aunt and grandfather, which my mother resented. Ma idealizes her father and thinks he is the epitome of what a man should be, which made Baba, in turn, insecure. Such is life, a chain of inane paradoxes and insecurities which binds us all and kills us in the end. Okay, admittedly that is not what kills us, but it renders our lives quite ridiculous, which is pretty much the same thing.

'Whatever your beliefs and ideas, you can't as a parent watch your kids play with fire,' Mashi told Omar and me when I visited with him last year. Omar was completely fascinated by her stories. His aristocratic family possibly view Naxals as exotic creatures like phoenixes that self-destruct. 'When I returned from England after my first year there I was still upset with my dad. But that was the year you fell very ill with measles, Sohini, and I thought of how our lives would end if anything happened to you. Nothing else seems important when that thought enters your head. You just want your child to be alive and healthy.'

I was somehow inordinately pleased when she said that. I was her child. This was before she got married and my cousins were born. She forgave her father for sending her to England just because I was ill. I haven't received much love from my father's side of the family during my growing years. Mashi's love means a lot to me. Even today.

I don't think Ma loves her sister's kids in that way. Or ever did. She just isn't capable of it. Her love for her husband and children is anxious and all-consuming, enveloped in a conventionality that borders on destructive. It left her with little time for much else all her life.

Now she has all the time in the world. Evil mother-in-law dead, children all grown up. I wonder what she's going to do with herself. Some social work, lots of lunches with random women she doesn't care for, and movies and lectures and seminars. She likes to be out and about town. I can't see Ma as an old person somehow. Can't imagine her all wrinkled and shrivelled.

'Don't let me fall ill and be bedridden. I don't want to live a life without all my faculties. Be ruthless and remove life support if the situation arises. Please. I would like that.' She has said this to Sudeep and me many times. She's one tough lady though. She'll be fine.

May–July 2005

Mrs Chatterjee

Working with Sanchita is not easy. She has never approved of my choices, which is rather hypocritical on her part considering she has always mocked me for allowing others, my husband and my in-laws, to make the decisions crucial for my life. Baba (she adores him as much as I do) made them for me before I got married and I made sure to turn them into the right ones because I had to make my life the best it could be. I am not a fool, I know how to be happy. And Baba did make the right choices – look at my husband, good-looking, intelligent and very successful too.

Sanchita thinks she knows best and that I'm a pushover who idealizes her family and is unthinking. But she is my only sister and when she needs help, who does she turn to but her stupid older sister? I am helping her run her school for underprivileged children now. I teach there thrice a week, my husband gives her advice on legal issues and we've contributed financially too, but it does not seem to be enough for her.

'Why didn't you come for your class yesterday?' she called and asked just now.

'I had a lunch party at the Saturday Club. Ruby Sarkar invited me; I had to go – her husband being who he is – it would not be good to refuse her. "You have to come, Mrs C," she insisted.' I laughed as I imitated Ruby Sarkar's slightly whiny voice, but it is a fact that I get invited to all the fancy lunches and parties because of my husband and it's important I attend them. He expects me to, and truth be told, I like going out and meeting talented, influential people.

'You should have rescheduled your class,' Sanchita said. 'The kids waited for a long time. Someone else would have taken the class if we knew you weren't going to come.'

Sanchita takes her school work too seriously. It is charity after all. My husband thinks social work is what rich housewives do to pass the time. I do not really agree with that. For instance, Sanchita is not wealthy though her husband, Arjun, is a senior bureaucrat. He is a good man, incorruptible, and therefore hasn't made too much money. Which is good, though I think Sanchita sometimes feels bad when she sees how easy life is for me, financially. Nor does she get invited to the sort of places I am always going to. I do the best I can for her. When I host parties and lunches I always invite her and, if it is in the evening, her husband too, but more often than not they do not even turn up. She will say she is too busy with her school to go out, especially if it is during the day.

'Sorry, I should have told you, I just forgot,' I said to Sanchita. She does manage to make me feel inadequate. I have to admit, I have been very forgetful of late. I even forgot about the ekadasi puja at home recently and the purohit and all the servants were shocked because I hadn't made any of the arrangements even though the purohit had given me the list a couple of days back. I don't know how that happened. I think if Malini started taking over some of these responsibilities I would be less stressed, but she won't.

In any case I didn't forget to teach the class in Sanchita's school yesterday. 'You know how your jamai babu is – so demanding. He was feeling unwell in the morning, yet insisted on going to work. I was running around, trying to make sure he was all right.'

'He is not six; a man in his sixties can look after himself. Why don't you just let him be? He can't enjoy this clucking around that you do,' Sanchita said, with not a thought for my feelings. She thinks it is fine to always speak your mind. Does she know enough about my family and circumstances to pass sweeping statements like this? What I do, I do for a reason, and I do not need to explain my reasons to her, even though she is my only sister. Her husband might not enjoy having her around, but mine does. Sorry, but that is the truth.

'He works around the clock – from nine in the morning to at least twelve at night. I think he is entitled to a bit of pampering from his wife when he is unwell, don't you agree?' I spoke calmly though I was really feeling quite angry.

'Get him another wife – there would be less pressure on you. You could share the pampering,' Sanchita joked. I found it to be in bad taste, but she persisted. 'Osama bin Laden has more than twenty wives for a reason. Anyway, don't worry. You'll come for your Friday afternoon class, won't you?'

Why would she bring in Osama, a wanted criminal and terrorist? Sanchita gets away with saying whatever she feels like. Baba used to find her random thoughtless comments funny. So does Sohini. Sometimes I just sit around while Sohini and Sanchita chat about matters that I can't relate to or care about. They can talk for hours. Half of the time they gossip about friends and relatives, which is of no interest to me.

'I must tell you Sutapa's latest,' Sanchita told Sohini about one of our nieces, a young and sweet girl. 'She has a towel fetish now. Wraps one around her head like a turban and another she uses like a cape. Then she goes around feeding the street dogs and quite majestically informs any neighbour who catches her eye that she is the Queen, taking care of the poor citizens of the nation.'

'At least the dogs get fed,' Sohini said, laughing so hard that she could hardly speak. Poor Sutapa has always been delusional but I don't feel it's right to laugh at her. I told them that.

'We aren't laughing at her, Ma,' Sohini said. 'Just the incident. It's funny.'

I don't see how the incident was separate from the person. My husband says only inferior minds want to discuss people and I have to agree. I have told Sohini that too. Not to waste her time on gossip. But she laughs and says everyone enjoys gossiping, let's not fool ourselves. Sometimes Sohini and Sanchita discuss politics and then they both act all-knowing, especially Sanchita.

A few months back they were talking about the elections that propelled Karzai to power last year in Afghanistan. I think it was when Sohini came down in January. This was actually a topic that was of interest to me.

'The ink they used was easily removable, leading to multiple voting,' Sohini said, and both of them joked about how the ink they used in India stays on till the next elections. I laughed too. 'But it's believed that the election results wouldn't have altered significantly even if one took into account a certain percentage of rigging, etc.'

'*The Kite Runner* is an amazing book – I had no real idea about Afghanistan till I read it,' I said. I had recently read the book and had found it to be wonderful. I was surprised to find that Kabul society used to be liberal and Westernized till there was political trouble in the country.

'You shouldn't form real ideas about Afghanistan based on that book, Didi. It's fiction!' Sanchita said and Sohini laughed.

'Still. Fiction also reflects real life,' I said.

'That's true too,' said Sanchita. I don't know if she really thought so or realized I felt bad and was trying to make up.

'The first hundred pages or so are fabulous but it gets too filmy after a point,' Sohini said. 'The end is all but ludicrous. He seems to want to tie up every loose end with a vengeance. But still, a good book.'

'Shall we go home now, Sohini? Your Baba will be home soon,' I said.

'Uff, Ma, let him reach before you one day – he will survive,' Sohini said, and this time Sanchita laughed.

'Okay, let's leave in ten minutes,' I said, though I felt like leaving then and there.

'Why are you always in a hurry?' Sohini asked.

'Because I have a busy life and many things to do. I really don't have the time to just chat like the two of you,' I said. I know they did not like it but it was true. I have much on my plate and I have never really enjoyed idling around for hours on end, gossiping and chatting. I had skipped my Loreto House Alumni meeting in the morning just to spend some time with Sohini. We did have a nice time. She followed me around as I did my chores and chattered away. About her art, her friends, Omar and his life. I look forward to her visits very much, I have to admit. Though I have such a busy life, I do miss my children sometimes. Even Sudeep, who stays in the same house but is too busy with his own work and personal life. Which is how it should be at this stage in my life. I am not complaining.

'Why don't you visit Mashi more often?' Sohini asked in the car.

'I visit her when I can. And we meet at family functions,' I said.

'Mashi was saying you stayed for just five minutes at Bhaidada's son's birthday,' Sohini said. 'You always seem in such a hurry to leave. Wherever you are. It's like worrying about your next activity is more important for you than enjoying the moment you are in.'

I didn't say anything. I don't remember attending this birthday party – but I must have, I suppose. I am getting older and my memory plays tricks on me quite often these days. It is perhaps true what Sohini said. I like to plan ahead, look at my calendar, check how full and busy it is. That gives me more satisfaction than the actual events themselves sometimes. I do have a fondness for high living, I will be honest enough to say. When my husband's clients and politically eminent people invite us, I feel a sense of pride. I enjoy myself thoroughly while sipping a good wine, listening to men discuss and debate politics. I ask some questions sometimes when I do not quite follow the conversation and they are more than happy to include me and explain current events in a simple way so I can understand.

Some of the wives have a lot to say. They interrupt the men with their opinions and ideas. I am not sure if the men approve of this. I find they usually try to politely include the women but I do not think they are taken very seriously. But there was this one party I can't forget. I would have been in my early forties. It was during the Sikh riots of 1984 or just after. It was in Dr Sengupta's mansion. There was liveried staff serving exotic canapés and wine. The men were discussing how the Sikhs had it coming and Indira Gandhi did what she had to and it was shocking that she got assassinated. Rita, a prominent businessman's wife, was sitting next to the folding doors that opened onto the garden. She stood up suddenly. She was wearing a black silk sari that made her appear like an extension of the night sky behind her.

'How can you say they had it coming?' Rita's voice trembled, she appeared terribly upset. 'Thousands of innocent people were slaughtered – it was a genocide and you say they had it coming?'

Everyone was quiet. The men who had been particularly vociferous shuffled their feet and exchanged glances. Rita had grown up in Chandigarh though she was a Marwari. She was different from the rest of us. Later I got to know that she had wanted to marry a Sikh boy but her family had bundled her off to Calcutta and got her married off in a hurry. I can understand that she might have felt bad, though I'm not sure making everyone uncomfortable at a party is the right thing to do. After a hard day's work the men were just enjoying their drinks. I remember telling Sohini about it the next day. She was sixteen then and beginning to take an interest in politics and what was going on in the world.

'I think it's good Rita Aunty said what she did,' Sohini said. 'Why should she stay mum while people talk nonsense about something she feels strongly about?'

'They weren't talking nonsense,' I said. Sohini was a soft child and easily felt bad for others. 'Men know about these matters.'

'I don't think the killing of innocent people can ever really be right,' Sohini said. But she was young then and she spoke tentatively. Today she would give me a long lecture on genocide, Indira Gandhi, the Emergency, sexism and what not!

The past few years haven't been as easy as I had anticipated. I had imagined that after my in-laws passed away my life would be my own, to live and do with as I pleased. It is not that my husband is a difficult man and he is hardly at home anyway. When he is, he expects me to be available which is acceptable. Two hours in a day is all he asks for.

'You can't teach an old dog new tricks,' I said to Sohini when we were talking about this. I have formed my opinions, moulded myself, based on what everyone, especially my husband, expects of me. 'It's too late for me to discover myself or what I really want apart from what all of you need from me.'

'I don't quite agree with that, Ma,' Sohini said. 'If you really want to, it's not too late. Ever. Everyone is pushing boundaries these days.'

I nodded my head but I was not sure. Or maybe I lacked motivation, did not really want to.

I can see the merit in any argument if you present both the sides in a reasonable manner. The world is not made of absolutes. Which reminds me. Apart from that party, I have one more memory of that year – the year of the Sikh riots. Aparna Sen had made a movie called *Paroma*. It had nothing to do with the riots but I remember the movie for other reasons. I also know I watched the movie the day after

Rita got upset at the party, so the two are enmeshed in my mind in a way that the Sikh riots make me think of *Paroma*.

Everyone was talking about the movie that year. Sanchita and her husband loved it. We watched it on our VCR at home, my husband, in-laws and I. It was an adult movie so the children were kept out of the living room.

The movie was set in a mansion like the one we used to live in when I first got married – a typical North Calcutta joint-family house, built around the central courtyard with the thakur dalan. I felt like I had been a part of the elaborate Durga puja in the thakur dalan that appeared in the first few scenes a hundred times. But when the daughter-in-law began an affair with the photographer friend, I felt uneasy – the way the relationship was depicted in the movie, as if it was not morally wrong, like it actually helped the woman discover herself. As though it is all right to do these things, they can be justified, can be explained reasonably. As I said, I am always willing to entertain different points of view and I found myself almost a little envious, wondering how it would be to totally let go, to live by one's feelings and urges to the extent that nothing else mattered. It would be heady and exciting but it would not last. What would be the point of indulging in an affair that one knows is doomed from the start? Or maybe one does not know that and hopes against hope.

'What a corrupt, disgusting movie,' my father-in-law said when it finished.

'Yes, these women like Aparna Sen think they are being modern but all they are doing is teaching ignorant women how to be wicked,' was my mother-in-law's response. For once she agreed with her husband.

'What did you think?' my husband asked when we were alone. I didn't want to tell him that the movie had confused me. I felt for a moment that he was testing me, asking a question for which there was only one correct answer in his mind. Which was silly, but I answered carefully.

'It's just a story. It was okay. I don't know why everyone has been making such a fuss about it,' I replied.

At the dinner table my in-laws vociferously lectured their grandchildren on upholding the correct values and not getting swayed. Sohini was quiet as she always was in the presence of her grandparents while Sudeep did not quite get what was being said – he was still too young. Afterwards, Sohini asked me if I'd hated the movie too.

'No, I loved it.' I was surprised to hear myself say that. I didn't know where the words came from but I did not try to take them back.

'Mashi loved it too.' Sohini sounded happy. 'Why didn't you say so when Thamma and Thakurda were going on about how awful it was?'

I shrugged. 'Let them think and say what they feel like. Why should it bother me?'

Sohini smiled. In that moment it felt like we were co-consipirators. I smiled back at her, suddenly conscious of how lovely it is to have an almost-grown-up daughter.

Sohini

In my late teens, I finally figured out how gender worked in our family. What I had till then considered tedious and silly suddenly seemed crucial. Earlier it was comforting to know I was not as valuable to my family because I was a girl. It just meant that I had been born into the wrong gender. It had nothing to do with me. Ma had always said it was acceptable because it reflected realities – that boys were more important to families than girls, and those who pretended otherwise were hypocritical. It was something I internalized and felt superior about – because we didn't pretend, other families did.

But I wasn't the one who got the last laugh on that one. I understood where I stood yet it fucked me up good and proper. It made me pathologically insecure. Knowing and understanding an unpalatable truth didn't help. It meant I developed a perverse preference for being treated as if I didn't matter. If anyone gave me attention, I felt it was because of reasons outside of myself – because my father was a successful figure in society or because they needed a favour from me or my family. I couldn't imagine that anyone could care for *me*; I could never be important enough for that.

Growing up, it was good to be rich. Wealth provides a natural cushion to the obvious manifestations of discrimination. In fact, it sometimes even gives the illusion of greater agency and equality. Wealthier women are nicely oblivious to how they are oppressed because it doesn't involve any deprivation except in conditioning which is rather clever. The word 'feminism' is anathema to them. Anyway, I got to do everything the other girls in school did (and more) simply because of all the money – tennis, swimming, foreign vacations, and so on. It won me envy which felt nice. If there was a deficit while paying bills at a group outing, I could always be the one to offer to pay up. Though there were instances when my responses to normal conversations or events were disproportionate and embarrassing. Like the time Susan was talking about how little money they had at home, yet her father would always sneak in an orange boiled sweet or a Phantom cigarette candy for her from the corner shack on his way home from work. I started sobbing and everyone was stunned and silent. But those occasions were few and far between.

And then I decided I wanted it. Attention. If I couldn't get it at home I would get it outside. I wanted something raw and primal that didn't involve thought. If I had to have sex with random boys and do drugs I would. So that's how I ended up spending my late teens and early twenties. The only good thing that came out of all that drugged-up fucking around was that my family (except for Ma) wanted me out of the city. Ma believed in me. It was what tripped me up every time.

Anyway, so New York it was. And soon my experiments with sex and scandal (or truth if Gandhi is okay with me euphemistically sharing his title) were over – they must have lasted all of two or three years at the most – and I studied hard for my master's degree and came back to Kolkata chaste and ready to start again. Which was the worst decision of my life thus far except that I realized it too late, when I was neck-deep in shit and trying to wade out the best I could.

I like to believe I met Omar when I was wiser, more sorted, less fucked up than before. Apart from being briefly attracted to his older brother (no, Omar doesn't know that), I really have been the model girlfriend. I do find Ashraf very charming. He is most dishy. Not a scruffy, ponytailed sort of person like Omar. Ma met Ashraf once and has gone on about how wonderful it would be if Omar too upped his game as far as appearance went. Not in so many words, but that is what she meant. I don't really agree with her. It's about being the best at what you choose to be. Omar does scruffy with elan and Ashraf does sophistication.

Omar doesn't mind anything much – that's his strength and weakness all rolled into one. I loved that about him when I first met him. It makes me impatient now.

He is too unambitious and carefree – it makes people like Ma uncomfortable, that he is content while others strive and strive. It's how women are supposed to be – happy and uninspired.

I was recently commissioned to design a map for children. I've always enjoyed working on children's books. The map book is an illustrated atlas, large, glossy. I loved working on it, though I don't see many parents buying it. It's super expensive because of the high production cost – envelopes with pull-outs, some pop-up art here and there.

Omar loves the atlas. In short, funny sentences sitting within colourful boxes and speech bubbles, I have described the political and cultural history of each region. He thinks it's a work of art. He wants to frame the artwork and make a collage for our study, but I refused. It would look so self-promoting or just infantile, the sort of proud statements parents make, forcing friends to ooh and aah in fake delight.

For some odd reason, it upset Omar that I didn't want it. 'What's the big deal? The stuff I design is all over the house; why can't we frame your artwork?'

'You design furniture, it saves money, apart from everything else, to use the stuff you make in our house,' I said.

'You don't like the work? It just seems the sensible thing to do, to use the stuff I design?' Omar asked. I didn't know he took pride in his work. It was good but also disconcerting to discover this.

'Did I say that?' I asked.

'You've never said you like my work, come to think of it,' Omar said. He made it sound like a sudden thought and I almost fell for it, but no. He had been waiting for the right moment to voice this.

'I must have ... I've got used to the stuff; I don't comment on it any more,' I said. I had never quite liked Omar's work. It was too over-the-top, a sort of kitsch that wasn't my style. Fortunately, he decided to lapse into his don't-really-care attitude at this point and I didn't have to dredge up any fake enthusiasm about his work.

Ma was delighted with the atlas too. She had been a diligent schoolgirl once upon a time. A map that dealt with history and society really impressed her as a work of utility that was beautiful as well. Though, rather uncharacteristically, she called me one morning sounding all hysterical.

'Malini has stolen all the copies of the atlas. I can't find any of the copies you had given me and I think she has taken them.'

'What do you mean by "stolen"? She must have taken one to show Sumeet. I will send a copy for him soon,' I told her.

'No, she has taken them away deliberately,' Ma insisted. 'Not only that book, but she is systematically stealing all your books, one or two each day. When you come next time, just take your books away. Keep them in Delhi.'

I was bewildered. Ma sounded like a senile, paranoid woman. Which is so unlike her. It was my grandparents floating conspiracy theories all the time. Who could have eaten all the mangoes? Isn't the petrol in the Maruti lower than it should be? Is the maid really unwell? And Ma used to flick every one of those away impatiently. She disliked unconfirmed surmises. Being positive came to her naturally, without self-help books and yoga.

The next time I spoke to her she sounded her usual self. She had given one atlas to Mashi and forgotten. The other one Malini had returned, saying Sumeet loved it and couldn't wait for his own copy.

It unsettled me a little, though. I wasn't used to irregular behaviour from Ma. One of the reasons I just gave up on being wild and wicked when I was younger was because of Ma's studious refusal to engage with the improper. Even if I tried to tell her what a bad person I was she would change the topic with platitudes like, 'Everyone lets their hair down sometimes.' Everyone but herself, of course. It was difficult to be bad if Ma would keep standing up for me. Even when stories of my recklessness reached Baba through some gossip channel or the other, Ma took it in her stride. She agreed with Baba when he suggested that sending me abroad for a few years might sort me out. And it did. She always knew which buttons to push where I was concerned.

Except the divorce, which she couldn't or was unable to predict somehow. Though she was always uneasy about the marriage, which was rather prescient of her. It was Baba who was excited when the proposal came. And I was going through good-girl phase and agreed readily enough. Okay, I can't put it on Baba alone. I must have wanted it too. I was attracted to Alok and the idea of a good marriage as defined by society. I wanted to make up for the badness of my teen years. I wanted people to say wow, she's married well after all. My reasons for marrying were dreadfully mundane.

It took me a month to realize I didn't want the life and marriage I had opted for. To enjoy love and acceptance from the social forces I had always despised had its charms but only for a bit. I wanted out. I didn't want to join the school alumni or a book club or a women's study group. I almost felt relieved when I realized Alok had an incestuous thing going with his mother. It was the perfect excuse; actually, it wasn't even an excuse. It was a foolproof reason. No one did a threesome with their mother-in-law. Ever. So I managed to get out and remain in everyone's good books. It was perfect.

I first met Omar through his girlfriend of those days, six years back. A pretty, vivacious thing who was also my colleague. She had invited us over for dinner. I was reading a lot of Rumi in those days and my first impression of Omar was that he looked like a sufi saint in his baggy kurta and untidy hair. I chatted with him on the balcony and we flung Rumi at each other till his girlfriend got jealous. The next day in the office, everyone was talking about how I had flirted with Sahiti's boyfriend. I told my closest colleague that I had found him attractive and charming and she told Sahiti who told Omar who told … I am not really sure how this chain ended but he did call me. Then life got messy – he broke up with Sahiti and before I quite knew what was going on, we were a couple.

It might have been messy and weird, but Omar and I were surprisingly sure of ourselves. It was surprising for me at least. I had been through enough crap emotionally and was eternally wary of getting into a new relationship. But it was different with Omar. I was swept off my feet. It also helped that I found him super hot. We knew we were perfect together. I don't believe in forever love but I know this is the closest I will ever come to it.

I was sure I didn't want to marry again though. Omar didn't seem to care either way. We belonged, we shared, we met each other's families and got along with them, but I couldn't imagine marriage. One of Omar's cousins had a wedding reception in Delhi a couple of years back – I was invited too. I didn't want to go. I knew it would remind me of all that I hated about formalized relationships. The inanities of tying two people together like cattle – it's actually done at Bengali weddings, knotting the girl's veil with the boy's chador or something. As a child, rituals fascinated me. After I grew up and especially after my own wedding, I developed an aversion towards them, particularly the ones that were so obviously rooted in patriarchy.

'It's a wedding *reception*. Just a dinner, no rituals, not a celebration of patriarchy,' Omar said when I told him how I found weddings unbearable. I still didn't want to go. But Omar's parents were coming from Lucknow and they expected me to be there. Omar's relationship with his parents was formal and respectful – he didn't question their authority while growing up. He didn't hurt and rebel. He was accountable for good grades to them apparently, and not much else.

I couldn't tell if his parents approved of me at all. Chances are they didn't, but they were nice to me. His mother is the epitome of graciousness. Statuesque, reserved. And the dad the way dads sometimes are – talkative, charming and slightly downtrodden.

I felt gauche at the wedding reception. I wished I had dressed up a little more. Omar's mother dazzled and shone, while I struggled conversationally as well. Theoretically, Urdu is my favourite language and it was a treat for the ears – the soft syllables all gliding around on the slick tongues of men in sherwanis and women in ghararas. I would have enjoyed it all if I didn't need to struggle to participate as well.

I loved watching Omar with his family though. The slight shift in his personality, the joking around with younger people and the adaabs and deference to the elders. He was so beautiful. He would make the perfect trophy husband if we decided to marry, which we hopefully never would.

'Did I underperform?' I asked Omar when we reached home.

'Were you performing? I didn't realize.' Omar lifted his right eyebrow.

'And now you are not prevaricating,' I said, feeling stupidly let down.

'No, Sohini. Underperform? Really? Sounds like a teen date question!' Omar laughed, making me feel stupider. One shouldn't need to perform for a partner's relatives when nearing forty. There was obviously something wrong with me.

'I just wanted to know if I didn't make a fool of myself in front of your relatives.' I wanted reassurance, and one might as well be direct if nothing else works as it mostly doesn't with Omar.

'You were perfectly charming. You always are,' Omar said. I wasn't pacified. Omar didn't believe in conversations that were unpleasant; he found them pointless. He often used flattery to get out. But that wedding reception was some years back. I am less eager at his family gatherings now. More comfortable, too.

But after all this time, it seems that Omar does want us to get married. Ma has been dropping steady, relentless hints for a while now. His parents have recently joined in as well. If he is not going to break up with me, we might as well be married. I imagine that is what they think. And Omar likes to do his own thing and keep others happy, all at the same time if possible.

I didn't hate the idea of marriage that much any more, but it's not like I wanted it either.

'I've been married once, Omar. It's a farce, I can't make myself go through it again,' I said.

'Your marriage was a farce doesn't mean everyone's is,' he said. 'For instance, I don't have a sexual relationship with my mother.'

'Yuck,' I said, thinking of his refined, regal mother. 'But marriage didn't *agree* with me.'

'Maybe this time around it will,' Omar said. 'If we are always going to be together how does it matter if we are married or not?'

'Will I really always be with you, Omar?' I asked, losing interest in the argument and latching on to the part I'd liked best. I put my arms around him tentatively. He seemed keen on resolving this marriage talk and I was very obviously trying to change the subject. He rubbed my shoulder absentmindedly.

'Let's have a baby, Sohini,' Omar said. I moved away a little so I could see his face.

'I thought we didn't care for babies,' I said, but I wasn't offended by the idea as I might have been a year or two back. 'I'm the wrong person for babies, Omar. I will be forty this year.'

'That's young enough,' Omar traced my lips with his index finger.

I don't know what it was. At that moment, I did want to bind Omar to me more deeply and eternally. Ma would say marriage and babies is the way, and I would've laughed and said, no, love is enough, and if it's not, it isn't worth it. But all of a sudden, I felt fragile, I felt the relentlessness of the years ahead of me. If one is a weak sort of person who needs anchors and ropes, then a baby could be the solution – the anchor that stops one from sinking. I wondered what the years ahead held and what a baby might mean for us.

Mrs Chatterjee

Sohini is pregnant. She is going to get married because she is pregnant. Omar's family wants her to convert to Islam so she is going to pretend to convert but not really do it, which is messy and worrying. It doesn't make much sense to me. I don't know how to break all of this to my husband. Sohini said not to mention to him that she is pregnant. Then how do I explain the rush? The wedding is two weeks from now.

I feel tired just thinking of it all. I am sixty-three now. I have spent more than half my life protecting my daughter. Sohini always struggled to understand why certain things had to be done. She was not rebellious as much as puzzled about the way the world worked. Her failure to be inherently conventional makes me feel guilty. As if I had transferred all my suppressed rebellions and inner turmoils to her. I never struggled like her though. Conforming came to me naturally. The rebellions and doubts I had were subliminal, deep below the surface of life as I knew it, not causing any ripples on the surface. I just knew they were there somewhere. Like a ship that has settled at the bottom of the ocean, old and harmless.

Though sometimes these days I get gripped by worries and thoughts that paralyse me for hours together. I don't know if any of them are valid at all. I try to talk to Sohini but she is so dismissive ('Don't be silly, Ma') that I don't feel I should be telling her. My food was tasting foul for some days. I felt someone was tampering with it. I ate as little at home as possible. Malini would keep asking me to eat more. She also seemed to be particularly attached to the new cook we had hired. Fortunately for me, our old cook, who has been with the family for over twenty years, returned in less than a month. Malini said the new one was really good and maybe we should keep both as Gobindo was getting old, but I refused. I spoke to my husband and convinced him that it was not necessary and he agreed. Malini and Gobindo never got along. Anyway, with the new cook gone I can breathe easy.

But now there's fresh trouble that I have to deal with as diplomatically as only I can. Sohini has been through many ups and downs in her life, though she doesn't like to admit it. It wasn't a biggie, she said recently, when I referred to her failed marriage and asked if that is what was stopping her from marrying Omar. I should be happy that they are getting married now, but I wish it wasn't because she is pregnant already. Though I am delighted that she is going to have a baby. This whole situation is so confusing.

After her divorce, Sohini changed a little. She lost her shyness and hesitation in front of people she didn't know. She spoke her mind freely. She reminded me more of Sanchita as she grew older. But she was never bitter. We shouldn't have pushed her to marry Alok. But no one can blame us. Excellent family, handsome, wealthy, educated, good job. I knew the mother was dominating but that was not the extent of it. The day Sohini told me that her mother-in-law knocked on their door at midnight and asked her son to come and sleep with her because she felt scared alone, I asked Sohini to come home and never go back. My husband wanted to speak to the family, try to talk it through. But I was clear that it was not needed. Sohini wouldn't go back to that household. Let Alok sleep with his mother at night. Sleep or do whatever else he wanted to with her.

Sohini had said that she never quite fell in love with anyone, so yes, arranged marriage was all right with her. In the two years she spent in New York she had a few relationships, she told me, but didn't like any of the guys she went out with that much. I didn't like the idea of casual relationships but I suppose it was better than her bringing a white American man home. At least that's what I thought then. Till Alok happened. Sohini had a bad reputation in Calcutta in her late teen years. She went through a rebellious, experimental phase which I knew she would outgrow. But it made my husband anxious and possibly that was why he was so very happy when the marriage proposal from Alok came along. I was uneasy from the beginning. Some sixth sense that unfortunately turned out to be more than valid.

And now Omar. I was delighted when she first told me about him. She sounded so very happy with him. I like him even though he has a ponytail; he is very good-looking otherwise. Omar is a designer of furniture and home furnishings which is a little odd as a profession I know, but he does have a degree from Cambridge so he is obviously very bright. I always mention that when people ask what he does.

The impression I get, if I am very honest, is that Omar is a little laid-back and lazy. I don't mean it as an accusation. It's just that I am used to my husband who is such a hard-working, ambitious man. As was my father. And Sudeep is very busy with his work too. But when I am in Delhi Omar joins us for lunch on weekdays and is always free to come out with Sohini and me. Sometimes he will go out for a meeting. Often he will be in his study at home but I hear loud music playing so it is difficult to imagine that he is working. I think Sohini sensed my discomfort because one day she suddenly said, 'Do you not like Omar coming with us when we go out? He won't if you don't want him to.'

'No, I love his company,' I said immediately and that was the truth. He is very funny and smart and I enjoy talking to him. 'It's just that I sometimes wonder about his work – you know – he seems to have a lot of free time.'

'So do I, don't I?' Sohini said. 'We work flexi hours from home, Ma. And believe it or not, we work really hard. Omar is in his study till early morning sometimes. His style of working is different, that's all.'

'He puts on music while working?' I asked. 'How does he concentrate?'

'He just does, Ma,' Sohini said. 'Why do you find it so difficult to accept that everyone doesn't lead exactly the sort of life you and Baba do?'

I quickly changed the subject before she got angry with me. When Sohini first told me Omar was moving in with her, I did get worried. This was around six years back. Since he stayed in a rented flat it made more sense for him to move in is what she said. I hoped he wasn't using her because she owned an apartment in Delhi. I mentioned to my husband that Sohini had met a man called Omar who she appeared to be in love with. I didn't tell him that Omar had moved into her apartment, but he got worried regardless and got his background checked. We were a little relieved when we realized he comes from a wealthy aristocratic family in Lucknow. His extended family includes many successful, well-connected people. One can say these things don't matter and we are being snobbish. But let's not fool ourselves, we all judge others by wealth and status. When I put it bluntly like this it sounds bad and I would never say this socially but I do make it a point to tell people Omar's family name and his uncle's name. Even if they are Muslim they have class, maybe more than many of the people we meet these days. Though I shouldn't be saying all this. The changes that are happening around us are for the better, according to Sudeep. So many poor, hard-working people have started to do well for themselves, make money. Being nouveau riche doesn't necessarily imply lack of class. It's just that new money is often accompanied by brashness and a keen consciousness of one's status. Still, it's a new world and it's good to see change.

I was eager that Sohini marry Omar and I am liberal enough not to care about religion. I know my husband found it more difficult to accept that at first, but he was pleased after meeting Omar. They got along very well. Omar is charming and cultured and, after two or three whiskies, my husband was particularly delighted to find that they shared a love for classical music in which Omar was remarkably well versed, having grown up hobnobbing with famous musicians in Lucknow. Our children aren't very musically oriented, which has been one of my husband's regrets. They listen to a lot of music but they aren't knowledgeable about it really.

'Very well brought up boy,' he told me that night. 'If Sohini wants to marry him I will have no objection.'

I was surprised when he said that. And proud of him. I made it a point to repeat it to Sanchita the next day. She might think he is terribly orthodox and unbending but he is actually a broad-minded man who appreciates intelligence and culture. And why shouldn't he? Being one of the most intelligent and cultured Bengalis of Calcutta.

Getting pregnant before marriage is something that shouldn't have happened. I was keen that Sohini have her own child and was almost giving up hope as she is nearly forty. But it's impossible to feel happy in the circumstances. I keep doing calculations in my head – it's June now, she is already five weeks pregnant, so the baby will be born in February. Even if she gets married end-June, everyone will guess that she was pregnant at the time of the wedding. The baby will be born less than eight months after her wedding. It will be so embarrassing. A baby should be good news, but I don't know how we are all going to feel about this.

'They are going to do a registration only and then a ceremony in Lucknow which his parents are very keen on,' I told my husband that night. After worrying the whole day about how to break it to him I decided to go along with what Sohini had said and did not mention the pregnancy. It would really upset him and even if he realizes later, I can pretend not to have known either. That is what Sohini suggested and, though I don't like to keep secrets from my husband as far as possible, this was necessary for his own peace of mind.

'Why so suddenly? They've been together for so many years now. Surely we could have all planned this together and better,' he said and I had no reply to offer except half-truths.

'They don't want any fuss or a ceremony, at least not in Kolkata. Sohini said she's had one big wedding here and refuses to go through with another,' I told him. She had said that, so it wasn't untrue.

'But we could have a small party for our close friends and relatives. Something elegant and nice – not a big extravaganza,' my husband said. It broke my heart. He has had to adjust himself for the children so much. When Sudeep married a South Indian, it was so disappointing for him. But Sohini had got divorced just before that and he didn't have the heart to express his disappointment at Sudeep's choice. He was very stoic and noble about it.

'I have made a mistake with my daughter, now let me quietly suffer whatever my son chooses to inflict on me,' he said the day before Sudeep's wedding. He didn't show his disapproval to Sudeep or Malini even once. I know it's not really true that all South Indians are dark – Malini's mother is as fair as my husband. But Malini unfortunately got her father's complexion. Sohini isn't very fair either but she isn't dark at all and she's always had flawless skin. You can tell by looking at Malini's skin that she used to have acne as a child.

'Maybe the next time they visit Calcutta we can just throw a nice party for them at one of the clubs,' I said. 'But should we go to Lucknow? Omar's parents are expecting us to come.'

'But have they phoned and invited us?' my husband asked quietly.

'Not yet,' I said. 'But you know this can't be easy for them either. Sohini is older than Omar by three years. And he hasn't been married before.'

'I am not going to apologize for who my daughter is. And I want to know if they are expecting her to convert to Islam,' he said. He is a man of the world. He knows how things work.

'What she said was they are keen for her to convert but Omar is not. So Sohini might pretend that she has converted though she actually won't.' Even as I said it I knew it sounded rather contrived. I really don't know what her plans are.

'She might as well convert then for all I care.' I could see he was getting agitated. This wouldn't be good for his health. We are all getting old. 'If the world thinks she has converted how does it help if only you, me and the two of them know she hasn't. What will we tell everyone in Calcutta?'

He was asking the right question – what will we tell people? I hadn't asked Sohini that. My head was hurting. I wish life was easier. When the children were small, I used to so look forward to them growing up and becoming independent, almost the same way I looked forward to my in-laws dying. And when the in-laws died I was too tired to rejoice. Their absence didn't liberate me the way I had expected it to. Same with the children. Changing soiled diapers was easier than dealing with the invisible weight of the emotional shit (excuse my bad language but I am simply extending the metaphor) that the children give us and will probably continue to till the day we leave this world.

Sohini

I don't quite regret it but we could have gone about this better. I was literally toying with the idea of what a baby could even mean and it just happened. Bollywood heroines in the 1970s and 1980s used to get unfailingly pregnant as soon as they lost their virginity – my favourite was the picturization of 'Roop tera mastana', with Sharmila Tagore wrapped in an enticing towel exchanging coy, lustful looks with a very horny-looking Rajesh Khanna. I was scarred and fascinated in equal parts by that song as a child. Omar and I can give them a run for their money as far as fertility is concerned. I'm not claiming the virginity part. Just sex without protection for the first time and wham, I was pregnant. So stupid of us.

'Do we consider abortion at all?' I asked Omar after the pee test in the bathroom. Twice.

'No,' he said. 'We should consider marriage.'

'Marriage and baby, all in eight months. Too much, no?' I said.

'Do you really want to consider abortion?' Omar counter-asked. I thought of Sumeet as a newborn, wrinkled and lovely. Till recently my love for children had been abstract, untinged with longing. But lately not so much. I imagined how hot Omar would look with one of those ridiculous baby carriers strapped on him with our four-month-old in it.

'You will be such a cool dad, Omar,' I said.

'And sexy,' he added.

'Yes, very.' I smiled at him. Ashraf was in Delhi on work and staying with us for a couple of days. We broke the news to him when he came home. Ashraf is two years younger than Omar but has been married for eight years and has two boys – six and four. They are quite gorgeous too. The world is full of beautiful babies. It's a trap as I've always suspected and now fallen into.

Ashraf didn't look particularly surprised. Just raised one eyebrow. That's what I like about these brothers. They are so calm and unflappable.

'Get a registry done pehle. Then break it to Abba and Ammi gently – along with the news of the pregnancy,' he suggested. We would have to get married under the Special Marriage Act. Omar got out his laptop so we could check it out on the net.

'Listen to this,' said Omar, going through the document. 'One of the conditions is that neither party can be an idiot or a lunatic at the time of registration.'

'So, if you can't get married according to the laws of this land there's no point in discussing this, is there, Omar?' I said and Omar threw his pen at me.

'I could've got hurt, you idiot,' I said lovingly.

'I would never hurt the would-be mother of my child,' he replied, crossing his hands and placing them over his heart.

'I'm glad you guys are enjoying this but I'm getting a little nervous about Ammi–Abba,' Ashraf said.

'We are panicking, Ashraf. The banter you're witnessing is tinged with hysteria,' I said.

'OH MY GOD,' said Omar, banging his head on the wall next to him. 'Ammi. Abba. What will they say when they find out about the pregnancy? Do you think they will guess we've had s-e-x?'

And all three of us started laughing and there was no stopping us. It was definitely hysteria.

The next two weeks were horrible. Telling the parents, watching them grapple with disappointment. Baba was the only one who was spared the news. He would have drowned himself in a bucket of water if he had found out. Or a glass of whiskey. Ma acted all virtuous about how she wasn't telling him for his own sake. But it was mainly because she wouldn't have been able to deal with his angst.

Omar's parents insisted on a wedding in Lucknow. Apparently, they lead very important social lives and they wouldn't be able to hold up their heads in public if their older son got married secretly in Delhi. Then his Ammi said what I'd been expecting all along. No marriage without conversion. Which makes me sound like currency, the permanently falling rupee which I can somewhat identify with. I knew what was being said though I could only hear Omar's side of the conversation on the phone.

'Ammi, I can't ask her to do that ... No, it can't be the only way ... It's just ... put yourself on the other side please; would you give up your religion for ... okay, okay.'

Omar put the phone down and looked at me helplessly. I put a hand over my stomach as I've seen many pregnant women do. It seemed a fitting gesture. If I wasn't pregnant all this wouldn't have happened. But I still couldn't regret it somehow. Omar and I had discussed baby names last night. I didn't want to undo the last seven or eight weeks at all except perhaps the conversation Omar just had with his mom.

I'd been to Omar's family home in Lucknow two years ago. It was not as alienating as I had expected it to be. Their house reminded me of my father's ancestral home in North Calcutta. Except that our old house is crumbling and decayed with some poor relatives tucked away here and there, while they live in theirs and it is better maintained and more opulent.

Our ancestral home has one large central courtyard with arched columns around which the three-storeyed house is built, sort of looming and red. Omar's house has many internal courtyards and high-ceilinged rooms – drawing, dining and banquet rooms decorated in a late Victorian style with French and English furniture. I spent a lot of time sketching while I was there, which made me appear more touristy than I had wanted, but there were some painted walls with a stucco finish around the archways and doors which I couldn't resist. There was a generous amount of open spaces, sudden balconies and alcoves, and lots of natural light in the house which I loved.

I was kept away from the relatives, which was a relief, and was given a room far away from Omar's. His mother spent a lot of time explaining, in an apologetic-assertive sort of way, how Omar's dad and she were liberal people but word got around in those places and the nature of their link to the larger community made it imperative that appearances were maintained and their social capital didn't get frayed in any way. Those weren't the words she used, they were more elaborate, and in a mixture of English and Urdu, with examples thrown in for good measure of people overstepping social lines and suffering.

I listened to her speak and was so reminded of Ma, the same doublespeak, the sense of pride and belonging laced with discomfort and awareness of being out of step with the times.

I told her that I understood and that my family in Calcutta were in many ways similar to theirs. She seemed relieved, surprised, even pleased with me, which made us bond in a way that I hadn't quite expected. I have always been charmed by her and felt awkward and gauche in front of her flawless beauty and Lucknawi graciousness.

Omar was a different person in Lucknow. I have never been aware of gender around him except in that city. It was the ease with which he slid into the surroundings that surprised me the most. All of us do that to some extent when we go home but his submission was more complete.

As a girl child I was and still always am aware of the imbalances, of the subtle ways in which I was never allowed to fully belong. I am happy to be in Calcutta, but after a while I find it stifling, the fact that I am not welcome in the house that I grew up in, in an absolute sense. Everyone is thrilled to see me, my favourite silvana is ordered from Flury's, I drip nostalgia in New Market and Park Street, but I am a guest, not a member of the family in the way Sudeep is. That's how I recognize Omar's sense of entitlement in Lucknow; it's exactly like Sudeep's in Calcutta. The male child's absolute rule in the house he was born in. I wonder why Omar left the city that bestowed privileges on him unquestioningly. But then we all know that the expectations that come with entitlement can be enormous. I don't think Sudeep or Omar can ever feel as free as I do, wherever in the world they may live. Guilt at the inability to fulfil unrealistic expectations is the prerogative of the male child.

I was left alone with the women, Omar's mother and sister-in-law, while the men went off to do men stuff. On Friday, Omar, Ashraf and their Abba went to the mosque to offer prayers. 'For form's sake,' Omar said with a shrug, pretending to be slightly uncomfortable. His mother said women did not have to go – you are not being excluded because of religion being the subtext. As if gender exclusion is totally fine. And while it isn't theoretically, I have to admit that at many levels most of us do accept it unquestioningly. It's something that happens in families across the world in differing degrees. Religion within a family, on the other hand, is rarely diverse, so the exclusionary practices of religion don't quite bother us in our daily lives.

Then there were times when Ammi, Ashraf's wife and I left the men alone and went off to do women stuff. Shopping, that is. Except that Omar phoned as we were leaving and said he wanted to come too. He enjoys shopping much more than I do, down to bargaining and choosing the right colours and fabrics. It embarrasses and pleases his mother in turns, Omar's efficient and keen interest in jewellery and fabric.

It was December then. Omar said his sister-in-law used to look appalled at the amount I ate. Ayesha is frail and delicate and pecks at her food so prettily. His mother was pleased with my healthy and inquisitive appetite. She is an awesome cook and very fond of feeding people.

It seems a little frivolous to focus on the seasonality of food at this point but I wonder if the summer delicacies at our wedding will be as gorgeous. We ate qalias, kormas and saalans of various types, raan kabab, murgh mussallam, shaamis and galautis. I dreamt of the food for months afterwards. The aromatic matar pulao we ate was a winter speciality too, as was the sagpehta served with mushy rice.

'Are you serious? It's what you will eat at our wedding that is uppermost on your mind right now?' Omar threw back his head and laughed with such delight that I wondered if he thought I was trying to be funny. I wasn't.

'You won't understand. You are too skinny,' I said.

'Pregnant women are supposed to feel nauseous and not interested in food,' he said. 'Especially pregnant women who are unmarried.'

'They are supposed to develop cravings for certain types of food,' I said. 'Pregnant women, even the unmarried ones.'

'Doesn't sound right.' Omar shook his head at me. 'Unmarried pregnant women are supposed to be consumed by guilt and praying for forgiveness 24/7.'

'In a mosque or in a mandir?' I asked. It didn't come out funny as I had intended. Omar looked unhappy.

'Don't. It's okay. We will see.' I wrapped my arms around his waist. Omar kissed the top of my head and stroked my hair. I felt young and helpless, which was ridiculous.

I am an atheist. Does it matter what religion I belong to? Or which god I don't believe in? As a Hindu, do I specifically reject Hindu gods? So, if I convert to Islam, will it also imply a special grand rejection of Allah? I have no idea and I'm too tired to care.

'Don't worry, Sohini, we will decide what is to be done, no one else,' Omar said bravely and rather ambiguously.

'Why are we stuck in a B-grade Bollywood movie plot from the 1980s, Omar? Unmarried pregnant woman, families putting pressure. Typically, I should throw myself off a bridge. I remember that happening in one movie I watched in a theatre called Menaka with some older cousins, in Class 7 or 8,' I said.

'No, that's awful. I think let's settle for your child being wrenched away from you after birth when you are too weak to resist. After years of toiling you will meet him again when he is a famous doctor and saves your life,' offered Omar. 'You will be white-haired and withered while I will be living with our son, alone in a haveli, and repenting the way I let my family ruin my life.'

'I am withered and white-haired already, so doesn't work,' I said.

'True,' Omar agreed readily.

'You are supposed to say no, you're not,' I said, a little annoyed.

'No, you're not. You are beautiful and flawless,' Omar said. 'And wonderfully stubborn and no one can make you do anything you don't want to.'

Except that I don't know how to separate what I want to really do from what is easiest. I like short-term fixes and non-confrontational solutions. I could convert to Islam and spend the rest of my life not thinking about it. Like going for a birthday party that doesn't leave a lasting impression. And perhaps my parents needn't know? Don't know if that's an option.

The way I look forward to this child confuses me. It was almost like peeing on that stupid piece of plastic made all the difference in the world. I would have been so relieved if I hadn't tested positive. I am sure of that. But the reverse didn't happen either. I wasn't devastated at being pregnant. It's hard to beat the conditioning that has been drilled into our DNA for centuries. Babies must be had – they complete our lives. I hate the idea of it, of succumbing so easily after all those arguments with Ma and various friends. What earthly good do we do by bringing more snotty babies into this wretched world?

I have seen how my mother has struggled because of her children. She was always a strong woman but now I sometimes feel she's on the brink, standing on a parapet and gazing at a void. I hope I haven't exhausted her infinite reserves of patience and sanity after all these years. The other day she asked me if it was time for my delivery!

'I am still in my first trimester,' I said. 'Whatever do you mean?'

'Oh sorry.' She laughed. 'So stupid of me. I suddenly thought the baby was due any day now.'

It was disconcerting but I managed to rationalize. That is what I always do. Stretch logic and reason till everything is accounted for and I feel comfortable. Perhaps, like me, Ma wants the next few months to pass quickly. That is what I thought. I want us to take the decisions we need to take about the wedding without too much angst, and once they are taken to have no regrets.

And then I want to live happily ever after, though I can't imagine it. I can't imagine a baby that will grow to be five and ten and fifteen and twenty. The idea itself is like a miracle, like saints levitating and the parting of the Dead Sea or was it the Red one? In 2012 the baby will be six years old. Six-year-olds can talk, argue, go to school, read and eat spaghetti. 2012 is not even that far away but I can't imagine life in that year even though I try hard. All I want is for the uncertainties to get resolved and then perhaps I will be able to imagine it all. Life with a child, with Omar as a husband, all that sort of crap.

October–December 2012

Mrs Chatterjee

I have a difficult time saying the name – Shazia. I have a difficult time handling her too. She is such a strong-willed child. I suppose when you have a child at forty, it is a different experience from having one at twenty-three like I did. Sohini does not like it when I comment on her parenting style. We have always disagreed on certain topics but not to this extent. She gets so uptight when I point out what she is doing wrong.

'You have to tell her what to do. She isn't old enough to decide on her own,' I said to Sohini when she was asking Shazia when she wanted to take her bath. A child needs to be told what to do and when. That is how they learn discipline.

'It's okay. Let her learn to take decisions. She is five years old.' I could see Sohini was getting angry with me. This has been the pattern for the last five years. Shazia is a beautiful child with long, thick hair, untidy and falling over her face, because she doesn't allow anyone to touch it.

The other day I forced her to sit down and took the knots out. Sometimes she listens to me because she knows I don't give in to her every whim and fancy, unlike her mother.

Yesterday there were some groceries lying on the counter in Sohini's kitchen. It is an open kitchen and all of us were sitting in the adjoining lounge area. Shazia went into the kitchen and climbed on to the marble slab and took the plastic packet that contained some dal or the other and shook it. One can never tell what she will do next which makes me nervous and I find myself keeping an eye on her when she is in the room.

Omar was telling us about some interesting furniture he had seen at a farmhouse. I am really glad he married Sohini. He has proved to be a solid, trustworthy person. Then I saw Shazia crawl across the counter and take a pair of scissors from a holder that contained an assortment of knives and spoons.

'Should she be playing with scissors?' I asked Sohini softly but Sohini was listening to Omar and did not hear. I didn't feel like repeating myself.

With one deft movement, Shazia cut the top of the packet, overturned it and watched the dal pour out. I screamed. I suppose I didn't have to but I really was not used to behaviour of this sort. Sudeep and Sohini were very well behaved when they were small and so was Sumeet.

'What are you doing, Shazia?' Sohini asked, getting up slowly.

Shazia did not answer. There were pink lentils on the black marble counter, falling in a steady stream and forming a small mound on the kitchen floor. A complete mess.

Omar moved to the kitchen quickly and snatched the packet away from Shazia. She looked startled and then started shouting.

'I need that, Abba, I need it,' she screamed.

'No, you don't. You are making a mess and we must clean it up,' Omar said firmly which was good. But Sohini had to step in.

'Why do you need it, Shazia?' she asked gently. I wanted to tell Sohini that this was ridiculous. The child needs to learn dos and don'ts, one has to correct bad behaviour unequivocally.

'I wanted to see how it falls – like sand or like snow,' Shazia said, sobbing.

'It's dal. It falls like dal, Shazia, and stop crying,' Omar seemed annoyed and I was glad. Children have a natural curiosity that has to be nurtured but not in a way that makes our own lives more difficult or causes wastage and destruction. I know Omar agrees with me on this and Sohini does not.

Sohini held out her arms to Shazia and comforted her. Omar shook his head and started cleaning the kitchen counter. I was going to leave for Calcutta the next morning so I did not want to get into an argument with Sohini on my last evening.

'Sohini is too patient with the child,' I said to Omar when she had taken Shazia away to put her to bed.

'I know, but she really believes that is how it should be done. She believes the way we were all brought up, with so many restrictions, curbs the spirit of the child,' Omar said. He is always so measured. He had cut his hair some years back and looked very good with short, trim hair. But now it is shoulder-length again.

'My daughter-in-law, I will admit, has done a good job of bringing up Sumeet. You know … Sudeep's wife …' I wanted to say her name and suddenly couldn't remember it. How embarrassing.

'Malini? You forgot Malini's name?' Omar sounded incredulous and amused. 'Do you forget my name too sometimes, Ma?'

'No, no, I don't know how it happened … slipped my mind for a moment,' I said. I hoped Omar wouldn't mention this to Sohini. I have always been forgetful but recently it has got worse and I know it makes Sohini anxious, though she doesn't make a song and dance about it like Malini.

Malini has been hinting that there is something wrong with me. I told her it is just that I am getting older. I enjoy perfect health in every way. It won't be easy to find a fitter seventy-year-old. Malini's parents are both unwell all the time; she has to fly down very often to Chennai to be with them. Perhaps she is a little envious of our good health. It sounds terrible but we are all human. Anyway, a week before my Delhi visit this time she insisted on getting a doctor's appointment for me – for a general health check-up.

'Why?' asked my husband. He really is not very fond of Malini. 'Why should you suddenly go to a doctor for no reason?'

'She just insisted. In a way, what she is saying is not incorrect. After a certain age, regular health check-ups are good – to take care of early symptoms of any diseases.' I repeated some of Malini's arguments but I knew my husband would not agree. Neither did I, but I didn't want to disregard her completely – it leads to tensions later. But he is used to tackling all kinds of people and situations; it is not so easy to fool him.

'The more you think of these things the worse you will feel. Why go to a hospital where all kinds of germs are floating in the air unless there is a serious problem?' he asked. 'Digging around for illnesses just like that is totally unnecessary and I can't support it.'

He is correct and I conveyed what he said to Malini. I think she did not like it. Malini told me the next day that she had cancelled the doctor's appointment. Maybe my husband had said something to her too. She seemed hurt and preoccupied but also worried on my behalf which was sweet of her.

'I just wanted to make sure you are okay, Ma,' she said.

'I am,' I said. 'It is just that sitting at home all these years has dulled my IQ. I think I need to get out more, engage with the world, understand what is happening in politics.'

Malini smiled. 'It's not that you don't work hard at home, but yes, do what you feel like, enjoy your life.'

It is easy for Malini to say that. She does what she feels like because she does not have the kind of mother-in-law I had. Like I've said before, you can't teach an old dog new tricks. It is too late for me to do what I feel like; I am used to adjusting, compromising, I don't know how to be spontaneous. Would I have been allowed to go to an office even if I was as qualified as Malini? Would my husband have stepped in and helped with Sohini and Sudeep the way my son does with his child? Not that I believe in equal rights the way my children do. Sudeep is a good father, but he is a man after all, and it isn't his job to feed and clothe a child. I do not say that to Malini, of course. But I do step in when Malini is away on work or to visit her parents and I find Sudeep struggling to balance his work and the household. But Malini does not like me to help my own son and grandson. She thinks it is Sudeep's job as a parent to do as much as she does for their son. But I am Sumeet's grandmother and can't I look after my grandson too? But no. According to Malini, I should only enjoy my time with my grandson, not have to take care of him on a day-to-day basis. I suspect she says that because she does not want Sumeet to get more attached to me than he already is, but let us not go down that path.

However, I try to listen to Malini. I have always enjoyed going out. And when I am not busy with my women's groups and social work activities I visit Sanchita, though we've drifted apart even further over the years.

Sanchita and Arjun, her husband, were watching TV when I gave them a surprise visit the day before I left for

Delhi. Their lives are organized and quiet. Not a million things happening at the same time as in my home. I do think I would be a little bored if I had to live like that.

'This Terrorism List that the US has? All hypocrisy,' Arjun said, turning to me. I didn't know what he was talking about but nodded a little. He understood that I wasn't quite following and offered an explanation. 'North Korea has agreed to give international inspectors access to its nuclear plants and in exchange the US has agreed to remove them from its list of state sponsors of terrorism.'

'Sounds like bargains made in the playground between children,' I said as he was looking at me for support.

'Really! Children in the playground is about right.' Arjun laughed and I was pleased. I had made a comment on politics that made sense to Arjun who is very well informed on news and current events. But he isn't condescending like Sanchita who acts as if I know nothing and she knows everything.

'Malini said she wasn't feeling well yesterday. Did she go to work today?' Sanchita asked because she did not like her husband and me to have a political discussion.

'Yes,' I said, without elaborating. And added, turning to Arjun, 'What else is going on in the world? I don't stay abreast of events as much as I should.'

'Oh, the usual,' he said, his eyes back on the TV screen. 'Look at this, Sanchita, now there's been a revision to the number of civilian deaths that happened after the attack by the coalition forces in that Afghan town. Bloody jokers.

How do we even trust the facts being handed to us by the media if they change from day to day?'

'I have a lunch appointment at Calcutta Club. I should go home and get ready,' I said, getting up.

I walked towards the door and, as I turned the handle, Sanchita said, 'Don't use that bathroom, use the one by my bedroom.'

'I am leaving, I don't need to use the bathroom,' I said, opening the door. It opened onto the bathroom. I shut the door, a little confused. I walked to the other door, across the room and down a short passage, hoping it would be the main door that would take me outside.

'What is with you? Are you okay?' Sanchita asked. Arjun wasn't listening, his attention was back on the TV. I like that about him, he lives in his own world and doesn't fuss about people and ask if they are okay for no reason.

'I am okay. Bye.' Thankfully, this time it was the correct door and I was out in the corridor and walked straight to the lift. I felt glad that I would be in Delhi soon. I look forward to spending time with Sohini. I always feel best around her even though Shazia does make me tense with her nervous energy and wilfulness.

'I will be fine flying alone?' I asked Sohini that evening after finishing my packing.

'You have flown alone a hundred times; why won't you be all right?' Sohini asked. She was right. I have gone all over the world on my own and so many times to Delhi, too. What a silly thing for me to ask.

'It's Malini. She was asking if I will be all right,' I added quickly.

'Malini has anxiety syndrome. She should keep it to herself. You will be fine,' Sohini said.

I laughed. Yes, Malini is a worrier. And it was foolish of me to get infected by her worrying. I went to the US alone for my niece's wedding a couple of years back. The others who were going from India went earlier. I could not be away from home for two weeks like the rest of them. I had too many responsibilities here and my husband would not have liked it, so I went for only a week and on my own.

I wish I was not so impressionable. Just because Malini thinks I have a problem, I am almost developing one. I have never been fond of housework but I have run a huge household quite effortlessly all these years. Sudeep and Sohini say I would have made a wonderful manager in a corporate set-up. They just tease me but it is also a little true. I am very good at managerial work – in my husband's chamber every evening, there are at least twenty to thirty clients; the waiting room is always full. Then there are the stenographers and typists and his secretary. Tea has to be made and served. Sometimes biscuits and snacks if there are important clients. I oversee all of that through my husband's secretary who I have trained over the years.

I am beginning to get a little tired nowadays in the evenings. Recently my husband got angry and rightly so, because even though he had told me earlier, I forgot to organize snacks for some very important clients one evening. Ten of them, so there was not enough time to quickly prepare something when I realized my mistake. I sent one of the servants to get samosas and jalebis but my husband had wanted homemade Bengali food.

'Why did you send samosas and jalebis today? Greasy and horrible. It was embarrassing,' he said when he came upstairs to sleep at one in the morning.

'It was a mistake. I forgot that they were coming and had to quickly send Harish to buy whatever snacks were easily available,' I said.

'How could you forget? I told you last week and even reminded you this morning,' he said. That was true. He usually told me only once and I would remember.

'I was going to make beetroot chops and fish fry,' I said.

'That makes no difference now. This is the second time you've messed up in the last month. Maybe I should talk to the cook directly,' he said, though I knew he did not mean it. I doubt if he even knows the names of the domestic staff or what each of them do. The driver and guards perhaps, but none of the rest. 'Your mind is on your social life – lunches and plays and your alumni events.'

I felt really bad when he said that. It is true that I have a full social calendar but it is all because of him. I get invites because I am his wife. He is such a successful man that it is important for people to be in his good books even if through his wife.

'If I am invited for lunches and social events it is because I am your wife,' I said. I didn't add that I have taken care of this household singlehandedly for many decades, and if I am getting a little old and forgetful he doesn't need to act as if that counts for nothing.

'Do you really believe that?' he asked. 'You keep saying how so-and-so likes you because you are such a wonderful person or how stupid some other wife is. I hear you saying such things all the time.'

I felt tears rushing to my eyes and blinked them away. If I have ever said such things to him it is because he is my husband and I share all my thoughts with him. I went to a convent school and my social skills are impeccable. I like to meet all kinds of people and never gossip like so many other women do. My father was a successful man too, so I have always known how to conduct myself around rich and influential people. Forgive me for saying this, my husband's father was a nice man and he did have an eye for investments and financial matters, but he was nothing like my own father. I sometimes feel my husband resents that.

'You really feel like I am one of those women who do nothing with their lives?' I asked my husband now. When I tell him little stories about my lunches and the events I attend, or repeat something funny or silly I heard, he loves listening and asks me for details. 'It is true that people easily take a liking to me and they talk to me and tell me their secrets sometimes. But I will not discuss these things with you if you aren't interested.'

My husband is not the sort to give in easily. He could see how upset I was, but he continued to insult me.

'I am only asking you to widen your mind a little, read the newspapers, think about the world, not just what concerns your own life,' he said. He sounded like Sanchita. Condescending and superior. I wondered for a passing moment if it was not ironical that the two of them hated each other yet seemed to have the same opinions quite often.

'I do read the newspapers. I am not interested in soap operas and mindless Hindi movies like so many women I know,' I said.

'Yes, yes, we have already established that you are superior to all the women you know.' His voice was thick with sarcasm. 'In fact, I didn't read the papers today. Any updates on the bombings in Somalia?'

My mind was blank with regard to Somalia even though what he said sounded familiar. I am not dreadfully interested in Africa but I didn't say that. The way he pulled me down and made me feel stupid was unfair. It made me angry inside. I do keep myself apprised of world events. I love reading *Time* magazine. But my mind is not used to intellectual challenges because it hasn't been trained in that way. I have been a housewife all these years. My husband couldn't imagine having a working wife. I would have been a different person if I had been allowed to have a job.

Whatever he might say, I know I am not a typical housewife, like the wives of his colleagues. Widen my mind, read the newspapers, think about the world – that is what he said. My mind is more open and liberal than his but

I cannot say that to him. He isn't used to me contradicting him even though he is aware I don't always agree with him. I do read the newspapers but I am not one of those overconfident women with an opinion on everything from Obama to Rahul Gandhi. And I do think about the world in my own way and I know how to listen. It is more than what most people can boast.

However, if this is something he wants me to do I will try to do it. I will read the newspapers more attentively and set aside a little time every day to think about what I read. At the end of the day, I am the sort of old-fashioned wife who looks to her husband for guidance. My ignorance of international affairs (not total ignorance but not a very nuanced understanding, I will admit) must be irksome for an intelligent, sharp man like him.

When I woke up the next morning my husband's taunts were still ringing in my ears. Instead of wasting time in self-pity I asked the servant to get me not just the morning's papers, but last week's newspapers as well. I looked up the international sections and read that at least twenty-eight people were killed in five suicide bombings in northern Somalia. Somali officials were casting blame on the militant Islamic group Shabab which had been battling the transitional government. I don't know what the transitional government stands for, whether it's backed by the US or some European country.

I am impressed that my husband takes out time to note events of this nature. If he can do it in the middle of his busy schedule, so can I. I felt a little ashamed of myself. I should try to educate myself a little more. Though my husband only spoke of Somalia, I read other news pieces too. Thirty men were dragged out of a bus travelling to Kandahar and beheaded. How horrific. A Taliban spokesman said the passengers were members of the Afghan National Army. The Afghan government denied the claim, saying the men were civilians travelling to Iran to seek work. In my head, it doesn't matter who the people were. Killing can never be justified.

I read other news items that caught my fancy. I like reading about militancy and terrorism. It makes for interesting reading. Special Operations Forces killed Abu Ghadiya, a leader of the al-Qaeda, in a helicopter attack in Syria, near the Iraqi border. Abu Ghadiya had smuggled weapons, money and fighters into Iraq from Syria. All the details tired me. But I wouldn't give up. A little time every day is all I needed to keep up to date. Sohini and Sanchita would be impressed as well. I am seventy but I still have my spirit intact. It isn't too late to try to focus and make some changes that can only boost my own self-esteem and, more importantly, please my husband.

Sohini

My friend Arindam moved to Delhi, with his wife and kids, a couple of years back. We meet often on the weekends. Last Saturday there was a party at his house. There were three or four couples, including Omar and me. It was late and everyone was a little tipsy. Apart from Omar, who has recently stopped drinking alcohol, though he still smokes pot occasionally. Islam forbids the consumption of intoxicants so Omar, who is suddenly discovering religion in his forties, has become a teetotaller. Pot he insists is not an intoxicant as far as he is concerned. It tickles his creativity and gets him into a quiet and reflective state, so it's fine. Okay then.

Arindam's wife Debolina is very beautiful. Typical Bong beauty with large eyes, curves in the right places and thick, wavy hair. She's also much younger than Arindam. I suspect Omar and she are crushing on each other. Not in a big way but I can see the signs. Long hugs when we meet or say goodbye. Engrossed in each other's stories and laughing loudly and happily when the other one cracks a joke.

I don't like it. I don't like the fact that I don't like it either. Jealousy is so mundane. I feel like an animal marking my territory and feel rattled. But I do feel old and unattractive. Before leaving for Arindam's house today, I went to the parlour. Omar was waiting impatiently for me to return since he was in a hurry to get to the party. Excited about meeting his crush, I suppose. We dropped Shazia at Omar's phupi's house and headed off.

'It's only eight-thirty. Why were you hurrying me like that?' I asked.

'They said to come at eight-thirty, didn't they?' asked Omar.

'Yes, but that hardly matters. It's a party'

'I guess,' said Omar. 'You look nice.'

I was glad he had at least noticed. I had blow-dried my hair and was wearing a new flowery sleeveless dress which concealed all my unseemly post-Shazia bulges. Debolina, incidentally, has no unseemly bulges. Even after two children.

I tried my hand at flirting that evening but I was out of touch. Not with Arindam, he is my oldest friend; it would have been too close to incest in my head. But with two of his colleagues, I tried to be all animated and excited about all they said. To ooh and aah about the deals being offered by five-star hotels (they were in hospitality) was a challenge, but I did my best. But if my intention was to get Omar's attention, it didn't work. He and Debolina were too wrapped up in each other. I wonder whether Arindam has noticed his wife's infatuation with my husband and vice versa.

Omar was delighting Debolina with some of his best childhood stories. About his science teacher who had dyed orange hair in a bob but black armpit hair which amused the class every time she lifted her arm to write on the blackboard. She wore fragile sleeveless blouses and chiffon saris which kept slipping off her shoulder and revealing her assets. Debolina squealed as if it was the naughtiest story she'd ever heard. Over the years, I had heard this story many times at parties. Then the one about his best friend Asif, who had a crush on the science teacher (contrasting head–armpit hair colour notwithstanding) and made blank calls to the teacher's house only to get scolded by her husband. Those were pre-mobile days and blank calls often missed their target, explained Omar, making Debolina laugh again. Though it really wasn't that funny.

Ma was going to arrive the next day. I dragged a reluctant Omar home at 12.30 a.m. on the pretext that Ma was coming early in the morning and I wanted a good night's sleep.

Omar and Shazia were having breakfast when I left for the airport. Everyone on the flight was out by nine-thirty and Ma wasn't picking up her mobile, making me rather anxious. Finally she came out, escorted by some uniformed airport personnel.

'I had left my handbag on the flight so I had to wait,' Ma babbled apologetically, looking relieved and happy to see me. 'Someone went back into the aircraft and got it for me.'

'She couldn't remember where she came from. Chennai flight she said,' the uniformed man told me, not looking happy at all. 'Then she had trouble identifying her baggage.'

I looked at Ma worriedly but she dismissed the man with a wave of her hand. 'All the suitcases look the same, how was I to recognize mine?'

It was true that Ma was quite a scatterbrain sometimes but this was a bit much. 'But Chennai, you thought you came from Chennai?'

'Malini returned from Chennai yesterday. That must have been on my mind,' Ma replied. I let it go, I had other things on my own mind. I thanked the man who continued to look surly and took Ma's suitcase from him. I wheeled it across the road to the parking lot, dodging traffic and listening to Ma tell me how relieved she was to see me and didn't know why she had felt so confused and lost for the last hour or so.

Ma hated using the seat belt because she thought, rather irrationally, that it was no one else's business if she didn't mind getting injured or dying in an accident. After I had established that I didn't want to pay the fine for her not following rules, she reluctantly buckled up. I started driving and, once she finished updating me on Calcutta news, it was my turn.

'So as you know, Arindam and his family are in Delhi now,' I said, after telling Ma about Shazia's insistence on wearing only purple pants at all times.

'Yes, didn't I meet him the last couple of times I came here? I forget his wife's name but she is very beautiful if I remember right.'

'I am sure Omar will agree with you on that,' I said, rolling my eyes.

'Men like beautiful women. It doesn't mean anything,' she rolled out one of her gendered platitudes. I found them more and more difficult to stomach as I grew older.

'Why should it mean anything?' I asked sharply.

'I don't know. I was just joking,' Ma replied.

'Well, I am not joking. I think Omar has a crush on her.' That's how it was with Ma and me. However much she exasperated me, I had to tell her all.

'Well, that can happen. You are so busy with the child, you don't give him enough attention I feel,' Ma said. Her natural empathy was towards men when it came to marital problems. Despite her immense love for her daughter, as a woman doing her wifely duties I always fell short.

'So should I confront him about it?' I asked.

'Of course not; it will blow over,' Ma said in her infinite wisdom. 'It will help if you are a more loving wife. And take care of your appearance a little better. Did you brush your hair this morning?'

'No,' I said. I don't know why I confide in Ma. 'It is your job to look after all his needs. Then he won't admire other women,' Ma said.

'That's rubbish and you know it,' I said.

'Anyway, it's nothing unusual. Haven't you experienced admiration from men? Some men are always trying to have an affair. Thankfully your father is not one of them. Nor is Omar I am sure.'

Wow. I wonder about my mother's life. And was I supposed to feel apologetic for the lack of male attention in mine? I think about my parents' friends. I wonder if any of them propositioned Ma. They are in their seventies now for crying out loud. Eeew, as Shazia is fond of saying.

'I want to ask Omar about it at least,' I said.

'Why do you want to?' she asked. 'It is not important. He is married to you. Let it pass.'

Ma's two weeks passed in the usual way. We went out for lunches and shopping and met the few relatives we had in Delhi. She pushed Omar and me to go out, offering to stay with Shazia – our maid was in as well – which was actually nice. We went to an art exhibition at Habitat, and for a movie which turned out to be godawful. Shazia was no longer the clingy child she used to be. Not with me at least. She is surgically attached to the iPad and the TV, something I know I should discourage but don't.

The day before Ma left for Calcutta, she said, 'I didn't meet Arindam at all this time. Isn't he in Delhi?'

'You know he is. And I told you about Omar and Debolina. I didn't feel like asking them to come over,' I said.

'Omar and who?' Ma asked.

'Debolina. Arindam's wife,' I replied.

'Oh, what about her and Omar?' Ma asked.

'I told you – that I think they like each other?' I replied with all the patience I could muster.

'Omar is cheating on you with Arindam's wife?' Ma looked scandalized.

'Are you kidding me? I told you the day you reached – that I think they have a crush on each other. I didn't use the word "cheating".'

Ma looked a little anxious. 'I can't … it was something … he did …'

It was so strange that she had forgotten all about it. She is an immensely practical person and moves on quickly, but this was hard to ignore. 'I told you, Ma.'

'Oh yes, you did.' I could see that she was struggling to remember. 'Don't call them over if you don't want to.'

Malini has been trying to tell Sudeep and me for some time now that Ma's memory lapses are alarming. Sudeep and I don't see it like that. Ma has always been that sort of person. Not terribly interested in chatting, short attention span, and multi-tasking all the time. She is relaxed when visiting us but she is incapable of making her mind still for long.

Two weeks after Ma left, one of my Calcutta friends phoned. One of my favourite people, erudite and earnest.

'I met Mashi in Tolly Club. Is she okay?' Charu asked.

'Why would you ask that?' I said, though I felt immediately anxious. 'She was here a couple of weeks back. Seemed fine.'

'She seemed a little different to me. Usually if she spots me she comes over to chat and tells me the latest about you, Omar, Shazia,' Charu said. 'She asks after my family and all of that. This time I could see she was struggling to place me for a moment till I said, "Mashi I am Charu."'

'Oh,' I said. I couldn't think of what else to say.

'Maybe you could get her sodium levels checked,' Charu said. 'A friend of mine here – her mother was going through these memory lapses. Really bad, much worse than Mashi's. She couldn't recognize her own daughter. Turns out her sodium levels were too low. And now she is totally fine again.'

'Well,' I said. I didn't seem capable of going beyond these monosyllabic expressions. 'She is getting older and she seemed okay when she was here, but yes, maybe we could do that. No harm in a check-up.'

I said that without quite meaning it. Sudeep and I had been brought up to believe that health problems went away if you didn't pay them attention. Like beggars at red lights. You need to turn away and pretend not to notice till they give up or the light turns green.

But sometimes the symptoms keep returning till you can't ignore them. Then you have the French Revolution on your hands and neither cakes nor bread to offer! And if the prison gates are broken down, they will have to be mended at the very least. I asked Omar if he thought Ma seemed extra forgetful on this last visit.

'Well, yes, but I didn't want to tell you because you would have snapped at me,' he said.

Now where did that come from?

'What do you mean snapped at you?' I asked.

'We are all touchy about our families,' Omar replied, not wanting to get into an argument. 'You get defensive if I say anything remotely unflattering about Ma or Sudeep.'

'So do you, about Ammi and Abba and Ashraf,' I said, though I felt childish and petty immediately.

'I said that, didn't I? That we are all touchy about our families?' Omar replied in his usual quiet, non-combative voice which always made me feel like the guilty party.

'So anyway, you said you thought Ma was more forgetful because?' Since I had started it, I might as well hear him out.

'One day she couldn't remember that she was in Delhi – asked me if I wanted to go to Bengal Club for lunch. She also asked me if I had ever met her sister – I don't know who she thought I was. A few incidents like that but she would also realize her mistake quickly each time. I didn't want to worry you,' Omar said. 'I suppose she should slow down, but as she keeps saying, she loves to be out and about.'

'Yes, she just needs to be calmer and more mindful,' I said. I was grateful that Omar provided an excuse for Ma's behaviour that I could latch on to. 'She doesn't listen. She has a yoga teacher but half the days she sends him away because she has to go out for something or the other.'

'She privileges a busy, active life over any other version. Most people are drawn towards the spiritual as they get older, but not your mom.'

I know Omar likes Ma's attitude to life, but I couldn't resist a little barb, 'You are already going that way, aren't you, Omar?'

He shrugged. 'A little, I am.'

Omar kept the Ramzan fast this year. And he has started offering prayers every day. Twice a day mostly, though when I asked him he said he used to do it when younger so it's not something new he's embraced. He used to offer namaaz five times a day whenever possible in his teens.

'Five times?' I asked. 'Doesn't sound practical.'

'Not like I have to. Some days when I am at home maybe,' he said. 'Don't worry, I am not going to become a fundamentalist.'

It's not about becoming a fundamentalist. I struggle with the idea of religion, and Omar, though he never called himself an atheist like me, shares my beliefs. Or so I thought. He has been teaching Shazia and me Urdu for the last couple of years. The by-products of religion – the culture, the literature – are fine with me. In any case, I have always fetishized Urdu.

'Such a rich, aristocratic language,' I had told Omar in the first year that we were together.

'So says the zamindar buried deep inside you.' Omar had laughed. 'I will teach you if you wish.'

Though that didn't really happen till after Shazia was born. Omar wanted to send her to a madrasa to learn the basics, which is how he had learnt Urdu as a child.

'Not a madrasa,' I said, more horrified than I let on.

'They aren't all that the media portrays,' Omar said. 'They are centres of learning too.'

'Why don't you teach her Urdu yourself? And me. I did never get around to learning it,' I said.

Omar had looked at me quizzically. He didn't suggest sending her to a madrasa again but he did start teaching her and I joined them most days. She picked up much faster than me. When Omar and Shazia chat in Urdu, I can follow, primarily because of its similarities with Hindi. And when Shazia and I talk in Bangla, Omar can follow too. She is very quick with languages as children usually are.

Unlike Omar, as I get older I find myself moving even further away from organized religion. He feels the need to understand and justify his religion which I feel is rubbish. Why would you care what some idiots think and believe?

'It's not just idiots any more,' Omar said, and that I can't gainsay. Religion is once again playing a bigger role in politics and society in so many parts of the world. Omar has been closely following the movements in the Arab world, what is now being called the Arab Spring. Despots were toppled, there was a move towards egalitarianism in many Muslim countries. I know Omar was excited by the prospect of a more liberal Middle East. But ultimately it failed to live up to its promise. God is not going away from the Middle East any time soon.

'Am I Pakistani?' Shazia asked a couple of months back. I wish she had asked when Omar wasn't around. He was busy working on the laptop but his fingers stilled, poised like talons over the keyboard as he stopped typing, even though he didn't look away from the screen.

'No, we live in India. You are Indian. Those born and brought up in Pakistan are Pakistanis,' I said. Shazia nodded gravely and I kissed the top of her head.

'Why did you ask that, Shaz?' Omar asked.

'Shruti's dad said I am Pakistani,' Shazia said.

'How do you know?' Omar asked.

'Shruti told me.' She was looking at Omar anxiously with a child's intuitive sense of everything not being all right.

'India and Pakistan used to be one country before, so it's confusing. Sometimes people make wrong assumptions based on names and surnames. Since we are Muslims, you and I, and Pakistan is a Muslim country, they might think we come from there,' Omar said. I was glad he wasn't upset as I had expected, though his explanation made no logical sense. There must be a handful of Muslims of Pakistani origin in India! Shruti's dad is an idiot if he doesn't know that.

'Ma is not a Muslim?' Shazia asked.

'No, but when I wanted you to have my religion, she didn't mind,' Omar said. For a moment, I wondered if he was being sarcastic, but he wasn't. He reached out for my hand and squeezed it.

Omar's parents had been upset with my refusal to convert to Islam. I almost did and then baulked and found that I couldn't. At the wedding reception we had in Lucknow – there was no religious ceremony – their relatives assumed I had already converted and I didn't mind that. But everyone was delighted when Shazia was born. There hasn't been a girl in that family in the last two generations. Shazia is close to her paternal grandparents.

My mother was very good with Sumeet when he was a baby. When Shazia was a newborn, Ma used to come to Delhi often. I found the first few months of motherhood difficult and tiring. Ma would call from Calcutta and say how much she was missing Shazia and find excuses to visit us as often as possible.

That lasted till Shazia was about one and a half and started developing a personality which Ma found stubborn and wilful. And now Ma suddenly seems older, retreating into her own opaque world, maze-like and confusing. I think about what Malini said, about what Charu said on the phone. For the first time, I wonder if Sudeep and I are being delusional. I don't want to let go of this thought. I call Sudeep even as I am thinking about it and tell him we should get Ma to go for a check-up as Malini has been suggesting. I say it lightly, almost as if we should do this for Malini rather than for Ma. 'Malini is so needlessly and sweetly worried. Hahaha.' I know Sudeep. He will withdraw at the first sign of serious thought. Everything has to come with a dose of humour in my family. So things seem easy and non-threatening.

Sudeep has agreed to take Ma for tests. Rather, he will outsource to his wife. The advantage of coming from a conservative, gendered family is that the girl child doesn't have to feel responsible for her parents. It's the boy who inherits it all, emotionally and financially. And his wife, grudgingly in all likelihood, has to be compliant and dutiful. Comes with the job profile. Daughter-in-law of a wealthy, still-living-in-the-nineteenth-century family.

'Will you tell Baba though?' Sudeep asked.

'No, you will,' I said. 'I hardly ever call him and if I call just to talk about this he will throw a fit.'

'You could talk about the weather first, Didi,' said Sudeep.

'No, Sudeep, really, you are the son and heir, do your duty,' I said. It didn't go well as he told me, a little accusingly, the next day.

'Baba said I was trying to appease my conscience with this sudden concern for Ma,' he said, pretending to find it funny.

'What's with the conscience? Why is it clamouring for appeasement?' I asked, though I knew the list.

'For not meeting all his expectations, for my bad board results in the twelfth standard, for not following in his lovely footsteps, etc.,' he said.

'He didn't say that, did he?'

'No, he doesn't have to, does he?'

'No, but are you going to get the tests done or not?' I asked, tiring of this back and forth.

'He didn't say no so I will pretend he said yes.' That was a relief.

'How's Sumeet?' I asked. I don't lavish attention on Sumeet the way I used to any more. I suddenly feel contrite. I don't want to be the stereotypical mother who is too involved with her own child to care about all that mattered to her before the baby was born.

BC. Before child. A forgotten era.

When it comes to motherhood I have been like a teenager, angsty, unsure, hormonal. At least I used to be. The teens are characterized by selfishness and self-absorption, but surely and slowly followed by a graceful opening up of the world, a slow awareness of how others matter too. I am definitely coming of age as a mother; I want to reclaim my position in the world as pishi, daughter, sister, friend and wife. It is only as an artist that I have managed to hold on to all I had BC. Because of the nature of the job rather than any conscious decision on my part. Painting is my release. It is what I do when sleep doesn't come, when Shazia is in playschool; it fitted neatly into my mommy schedule and therefore it prospered.

'I am one of those annoying parents who is obsessed with their child, right, Omar?' I ask Omar that night, after talking to Sudeep. The thought that I hardly kept up with Sumeet was still nagging me. Sumeet was my first child, his was the only bum (other than my own) I had cleaned after potty. A million times. Shazia's little bum came into my life much later.

Omar put the book he was reading on his chest and his reading glasses on his head. So, this merited his full attention. He has had the reading glasses for a couple of years now and uses them thoughtfully.

'Not completely but to an extent, yes. You don't talk about it the way some mothers do so one doesn't notice as much, but it is your whole world now. Motherhood.'

'That's not true. I have been doing well professionally. How could that have happened if I was too involved with Shazia?' I had wanted reassurance from Omar, not agreement.

'You know how that's happened. Art can be made in isolation, at home – it has complemented your Shazia life perfectly. And I've done the rest – getting it out there, the sales and marketing part of it.'

These days I lose interest in the canvas after I am finished with it. If Omar didn't follow up, they would all be lying around at home.

'Shazia is getting bigger. I really did feel overwhelmed when she was small ... You were pretty much like me, obsessing and watching over her all the time,' I said. I was caving in, asking him to understand.

'Yes, you're right. I just feel I got out of that phase faster than you,' Omar said. And then you got into the Debolina phase, I thought, feeling irritated, but didn't say it out loud.

'She was born when I was forty; the only way I could accommodate her in my life was by changing it completely,' I said.

Omar shrugged. 'And nothing prepared me for the love. It sort of swept me away. I – I didn't know you could care that much for another being.'

'That is where I got left behind,' said Omar. 'The love I feel for Shazia is not exclusive the way your love for her is.'

'It's not exclusive.' I wish I hadn't started this conversation. Now he was putting the blame on me. He does that more and more these days. I wondered if I should take a cheap shot at how right he was about his love not being exclusive but decided against it. I chose to go with straight and serious talk. 'There are different kinds of love, Omar, it's the fact that we created her that is so amazing ...'

'Whatever it is, Shazia is top of your chart and you are top of mine,' Omar said. I didn't have an answer. Did I believe him? Was I really top of his chart?

'Are you jealous of your own daughter, Omar?' I asked, trying to make a joke of it.

'I wish I didn't have reason to be,' Omar replied.

'This is ridiculous, I can't believe we are having this conversation,' I said. I couldn't let him get away with playing the martyr. 'And I don't have any reason to be jealous of Debolina, I suppose?'

Omar was taken aback. I caught a flicker of uncertainty on his face. He frowned, but then his forehead cleared and he said, 'It's fun to flirt with a pretty, intelligent woman. It's enjoyable, but there is no reason for you to be jealous.'

Omar and Debolina's flirtation was conducted mostly through giggles and silliness so I wonder how he knew she was intelligent. But I didn't really want to go there. If I had asked, it was because I wanted him to stop attacking me. I didn't want to discuss her beauty or IQ. Besides, we had been together too long. The days of intense jealousy, tearful fighting and overwhelming love were over. And if he said I had no reason to be jealous I would go with that.

'If you say so,' I said, feeling dull and jaded.

'I do say so,' said Omar. He put his glasses back on his nose and opened his book.

I lay down. The room was heavy with misgivings and unspoken thoughts. But I didn't want it to be this way. And I didn't want to be this person either. Cynical, suspicious. I turned and put my arm across Omar's chest. I squeezed his shoulder. His muscles were taut and sinewy. He went to the gym regularly. He had always been a little vain, though when I teased him he insisted it was good health he was after. Yeah, right. I rubbed my head against his shoulder. He continued to read or pretend to read.

'When it comes to hotness you have no competitor, you know,' I said. I really shouldn't complain about his vanity when I was the one who fed it regularly. But beauty must be appreciated, in my opinion. Like every other achievement.

'Even of that I'm not sure any more,' he said.

'So, who is your competitor on the hotness front?' I was annoyed again, after that brief flash of love or vague stirring of lust. Whatever it was.

'No one,' he said. Oh. While I had to contend with Debolina what he had to battle was Motherhood!

'Then why did you say you aren't sure of it?' I asked.

'Of what?' He really wasn't paying attention. Or he was behaving like Ma.

'Of having no competitor on the hotness front,' I reminded him.

'I wasn't suggesting I have competition. All I was saying was that all the hotness doesn't get me much action any more, does it?' Omar was smiling now.

Was that all? The urge to disprove him was strong. I rubbed his thigh and kissed him.

'Pity sex, is it?' he said, refusing to be drawn in.

'Even if it is, you are unable to resist,' I said. It's unfortunate if you are a man with a traitorous penis that doesn't know how to feign indifference. 'Come on, Omar, I'm sorry. I love you, you know that.'

He turned and looked into my eyes. 'I have never taken you for granted,' I added.

'I don't mind if you do,' he said. 'It's just that … I feel like I can't reach you the way I could any more.'

'I am here; next time you reach out, I will be here,' I said.

Too many grievances. Had I really pushed Omar away after Shazia was born? 'If that is how you feel you should've told me about it earlier.'

'I have. You weren't listening,' he said.

'Okay, but I hear you now,' I said.

Omar didn't speak so I felt the need to justify. 'The love I have for Shazia is exhausting. It takes up all my energy, my strength. You are an adult, I thought this was obvious and acceptable to you.'

'I don't know, Sohini, I just miss us. What we had before.' Omar has a way with words. He knows how to use them to induce guilt.

'Well, Shazia is getting bigger and I have been thinking about these things … I've been noticing stuff … I do intend to be better at managing it all now, at being a daughter to Ma, a pishi to Sumeet, a partner to you, and everything else,' I said.

'You are not bad at any of it. I like watching the mother in you, Sohini, I never knew it was there,' Omar said. He knew how to induce guilt but he couldn't deal with it. That's Omar. I realized that I'd missed him too. Even while he was right beside me. It is possible to do that.

'I want us back too. I'm sorry, Omar, but I really do.'

'I'm feeling stupid for fussing, but I am glad to hear that,' he said. He ran his index finger over my lips the way he used to, aeons ago.

'That's okay.' I kissed him. 'You are good at being a parent. It comes to you more naturally than it does to me. In spite of it all. And I'm sorry.'

I didn't know in spite of what all, but Omar seemed to get it. He smiled and I knew he forgave me, if forgiveness was required. And I forgave him too. Just in case.

'In that case, you need to make it up to me now.' Omar said, cupping my left breast and I felt a rush of longing that I hadn't experienced in a while. 'I am sorry and I love you, too.'

Yes, I want to get it all back. I'm not seeking perfection or anything new, just the comforts and pleasures that used to be mine, that needn't come in the way of my relationship with my child. I am preoccupied and angsty in a way I never used to be. Besides, I am worried about Ma. I need Omar. I need him to be around and to understand. I don't think I am asking for too much. He is all I have.

Mrs Chatterjee

I got up and left the room in a dignified manner and refused to answer the ridiculous question paper. I do not know what Malini is trying to do. This is part of a health check-up? I have quietly undergone the blood tests, X-rays, EEGs. Even though I know full well nothing is wrong with me. I answered politely when the doctor asked me inane questions about time, chronology, and so on. I got a little confused about the days of the week but that was because I was flustered.

Since I was five years old no one has asked me such ridiculous questions. The doctor said 'very good' at one point because I was able to answer a trick question he was trying to fool me with.

I thought that would have been all, but then I was told to take a written test. I wrote some of the answers. I found my concentration slipping because it was so insulting, the sort of things I was being asked to write and draw. As if it was a kindergarten admission test. Therefore,

I walked out. Malini was sitting in the waiting room, reading a book.

'Let's go home,' I said to her.

'You've come out rather fast,' she said, getting up.

'Yes, because it really is a waste of time,' I said, walking towards the main door. The attendant came out carrying the paper and asked me to fill in my name on the dotted line at the top.

'I already did,' I said, pointing to where I had written Mrs C.

'Mrs C?' asked the attendant, smiling. He was more annoying than the doctor.

'Yes, that's who I am.' I had been harassed all morning and my mind was now blank. Mrs C was enough. Why did I need to write what it stood for? What did I care what it stood for?

Malini took the sheet from the attendant and filled it in with a deep sigh. I couldn't tell what she wrote.

'Let's go home,' I said to her but she headed towards the reception instead, mumbling something about letting the doctor know.

I stood patiently near the door. Malini gestured to me to wait and went into the room where I had taken the test. I wanted to go home. I told her it was a waste of time, but she wouldn't listen to me, of course. She wants me to be unwell and prove it she will at any cost.

I called Sohini from my mobile phone instead of standing near the door vacantly, waiting for Malini to finish whatever she might be doing.

'Hello Ma,' she said. 'What's up?'

'I don't know what game Malini is playing with me,' I whispered. 'Maybe she is trying to prove I am insane.'

'I can't hear properly, Ma,' Sohini said. 'What is Malini doing?'

'She is making me take all sorts of tests, to prove something. I don't know what.' I was still whispering, but loudly enough for Sohini to hear.

'Sudeep knows about the tests, right? So does Baba. Don't worry. They must only be routine tests,' she replied.

I didn't know how to convince her that I knew something is wrong. I had a gut feeling about this. I was not overreacting. After a lifetime of measured responses, I was not suddenly going to get melodramatic and excitable, was I?

It is not that I was calling Malini evil or anything like that. Let's be honest. I was not terribly attached to my own mother-in-law, so I can understand these things. But I also know that I have been supportive and understanding as far as Malini goes. I value goodness and decent behaviour and I would never hurt anyone wilfully. I really am nothing like my mother-in-law, everyone knows that.

I stayed quiet on the way home. I wanted Malini to sense my disapproval.

'Sudeep wants us to go out for dinner tonight,' Malini said.

'All right, we can.' I didn't ask when or where. We rarely go out for dinner together as a family, except when Sohini is visiting. I don't know why Sudeep had suddenly made this plan. But I rarely got to spend time with my grandson so I hoped he would come too. He is always busy with his friends and tuitions and sports. When he was younger he used to spend more time with me. He loved going to Science City and Nicco Park and I loved accompanying him. I took him swimming and for golf to Tolly Club during his summer holidays. We often had breakfast together at the club or at home.

He is thirteen now. But he still comes into my room and talks to me in the afternoons sometimes when his mother is at work. Lies down on the bed, says silly things to make me laugh. How much longer will he enjoy spending time with his grandmother? Soon it will be a reluctant duty which his father, my son, will insist that he fulfils. He will do so grudgingly and then, once I am dead, he will wish he had spent more time with me because he will remember how happy he made me. I want him to remember me, but with happiness, not guilt; I want him to hold the memories close not because I crave eternity – I am not that foolish – I just want my life to matter for one more blink of the eye. I want my grandson to think of me now and then, maybe when he eats pancakes with strawberries which we so often had together, or listens to an old song from my time. I will be past caring by then but it makes me happy now, just knowing that Sumeet will think of me, maybe less and less with time but never forgetting.

He is thirteen now. How much longer will he enjoy spending time with us? Haven't I said this already? Never mind if I'm repeating myself. It's the prerogative of the elderly, and I am not young any more. I don't know how many more summers I will live so let me enjoy this upcoming one, let me not think of tomorrow or the day after, just of this summer that I will spend with my grandson. I am not an emotional or sentimental sort of person, but sometimes these thoughts do cross my mind.

Malini was sitting next to me in the car, talking, giving me all sorts of advice. I was nodding and pretending to listen. Apart from giving birth to Sumeet she has not really been particularly useful. But I nodded and smiled. After all, she did give birth to my grandson. And how good-looking he is! The South Indian genes did not prevail, thankfully. I am not being rude, am I? Surely Malini is also secretly glad that her son is as handsome as her father-in-law? I am sure she is.

When we reached home, Sudeep was already there. I had lost count of how many hours we spent at the hospital. He asked what the doctor had said, but I brushed the question aside and instead asked him where we were going to have dinner. Simply because I do not enjoy talking about health. Especially when there is nothing to discuss.

'Baba doesn't like any of these new restaurants, does he? Let's just go to Oberoi,' he said.

'Unless Sumeet wants to go to some new restaurant or the other. He likes to go to all sorts of places and your Baba will never say no to something his grandson wants to do,' I answered.

'He really bullies the two of you, Ma. You shouldn't let him,' Malini said with a laugh. I wish she wouldn't interfere in our relationship with our grandson, but it is the sort of person she is. Too many opinions.

When I came downstairs after getting ready for dinner, Malini and Sudeep were already in the living room, waiting for us.

'Baba's coming?' Sudeep asked. The whiskey and ice bucket were on the centre table. Also, port for Malini and me. I love port as Sudeep knows.

Before I could answer, Malini got up and, holding my elbow, she said, 'Ma, just … your sari. Can I put it right if you don't mind?'

I disentangled my elbow from her hand but allowed her to lead me to the guest room. I wanted to tell her I did not care about these things – if my petticoat was showing or something trivial of that nature. But I am not the sort of person who can answer rudely.

'You are wearing it wrong,' she said. I looked down and yes, all the threads were showing. I might as well take it off and put it on again the right way.

'Thank you, Malini, but I would like to do it myself,' I said. I did not know why she had accompanied me to the room. She could have just told me what was wrong without making such a show of it, leading me out of the living room as if she could not say what was wrong in front of Sudeep.

'We can do it together – quickly,' she insisted.

'I can do it quickly myself, I wear saris all the time as you know.' She might need help with wearing a sari, but

I really don't. 'Why don't you go and have a drink with Sudeep and Baba?'

'Okay,' she said reluctantly and went out of the room. I started unwrapping my sari. I should be careful too and not give her a chance to point these things out. For me, a sari worn wrong is not something to make a fuss about. I have never been all that particular about how I look or dress.

When I went back to the living room my husband, Sudeep and Malini were sipping their drinks.

'Here, Ma,' said Sudeep, pouring me a glass of port. 'Sohini just called. She is coming down next month to visit you.'

'Oh good.' I was pleased. 'Is she going to have an exhibition here?'

'I don't know … she didn't say.'

'With Shazia and Omar?' I asked. I hope they are coming together. In Calcutta, people will wonder if everything is all right with their marriage if Sohini visits without Omar too often. Besides, I like taking Omar and Shazia around. Omar is such a charming boy, he makes everyone laugh. And everyone is now used to him being Muslim, so I don't get the barrage of questions I used to earlier from our friends and relatives. You know, about whether he eats pork, drinks alcohol and whether Sohini converted to Islam. I suppose people were just curious but it was tiring and some of the questions would be a little malicious. Not everyone's, of course, just people like Mridula and Nandini who are famous for being hurtful and snobbish.

When Jayanta and Minakshi's daughter married a person from a lower-middle-class Bengali home – a very educated boy brought up in Midnapore – Mridula deliberately spoke in English to the boy's parents at the wedding. Even as they stuttered and answered in Bangla she continued to talk in English. I don't know what pleasure it gave her to behave in that way. But Omar was not intimidated by their bullying ways. I was delighted with the way he fended off Mridula and Nandini the first time they met him.

'So have you ever been to a madrasa?' Nandini asked Omar when I introduced them. After some polite chitchat this is what she asked, arching her eyebrows as if it was such an intelligent question.

'Yes, I used to learn Urdu at a madrasa as a child.' Omar was not ashamed of his upbringing. Why should he be? He comes from a much more cultured background than Nandini's. And in any case, everyone knows the sort of reputation her husband has in business circles.

'How quaint,' said Mridula. 'But is it safe to study in a madrasa?'

'Not at all,' replied Omar. 'Every now and then a child would be dragged away by the Taliban recruits who hung around while we did our lessons.'

Mridula and Nandini looked stunned for a moment. Omar smiled and said, 'But I wasn't one of those kids. I lived to marry a beautiful Bengali girl and meet all of you lovely ladies.'

They realized he was teasing and felt a little sheepish, I could tell. They also found him charming. Whenever I meet them now they ask when Omar will visit next. They are the sort of women who are merciless if they find someone weak, but submissive and flirtatious when the person gives it back to them. Sounds crude, but they are not the sort of people who deserve consideration and understanding.

'Omar's fan club,' Sohini and I tease him. Not just Mridula and Nandini but a lot of our family and friends, both men and women.

'I should come here more often, Ma,' Omar told me once. 'I thought it was only Sohini, but it seems all Bengali women fancy me. I love it.'

'I will be very happy if you come more often, for whatever reason,' I said. I meant it too. As I get older, I don't enjoy socializing the way I did. I want my children and grandchildren around. And that is enough. The last time I met Mridula I felt disgusted. Earlier I thought her to be humorous, even though she was mean and sarcastic. But I find the humour grating on my nerves now.

'Anita di, why didn't you come for the cooking demonstration yesterday?' Mridula asked me a few days back.

'Where?' I asked her.

'What is happening to you these days? You keep forgetting everything. You need to relax. Is Ranjan da keeping you up all night?' Mridula nudged Seema who was standing next to her and they both laughed. I thought the joke was not in good taste at all.

'I was busy. Malini wanted me to go with her ...' I said. I had forgotten about the invite actually, but I did not want to say that.

'Forget about your daughter-in-law. It's your son-in-law we all want.' Again she laughed. Again a tasteless joke. 'I thought you would come for the demo though – it was so good. The pastries were fabulous. But then, she is a chef, a professional; I was lucky she agreed to come and give us lessons.'

Suddenly I remembered. I like baking and it would have been nice to have learnt something new to cook for Sohini when she visited.

'I forgot about the cookery class. Would have tried to squeeze out time ... I really did want to attend it,' I said. I was being honest but it is not always a good idea to be open and frank in front of people like Mridula.

'You forgot? I called you and reminded you the day before. How could you forget? I don't think I should joke about it. Are you all right?' Mridula pretended to be concerned though I knew it was fake.

'Oh, I'm fine. Tell me more about the class and what you learnt.' I tried to change the subject but she would not let it go. She called out to Nandini and told her, dramatically with a grimace, that I forgot to attend the session. She put an arm around my shoulder. I felt like pushing it off but I can never be rude to anyone.

I continued to feel annoyed even after I got home. I am tired of people asking after my health all the time. I do not remember the last time I had a fever or any illness of any sort. I asked my maid to get me a cup of tea and the newspaper. I didn't want to have stupid thoughts in my head. My husband was right – it is best to keep the mind open and alert to all that is going on in the world instead of focusing on what people like Mridula are saying. What a waste of time that would be.

I like reading the newspapers. So much happening in the world. New discoveries and inventions every day. Remarkable. There are tragedies too, of course. They give us a perspective on how lucky we are. Though I feel people worry about the environment a little too much nowadays. 'Adaptation to climate change is urgent and must be part of development,' said Bárbara Pesce-Monteiro, the United Nations resident coordinator in Cuba, assessing the damage done by hurricane Sandy in the eastern region of the country. I read this and shake my head. Hurricanes have been around forever. I don't see how they have anything to do with climate change. Sohini and Omar won't agree with me, of course. I have heard them discussing climate change very seriously.

I miss Sohini. I really want to be with her. More than with anyone else. I feel most peaceful when I am with her. I wish she lived in Calcutta. Even though people say it's a dead city. She is a successful artist now. I am so proud of her. If she had stayed in Calcutta she might not have had all the opportunities she has had in Delhi. I am glad she is there, though I also wish she was here. Never mind. I can visit her as often as I like. And she can come too whenever she is free.

Sohini

The R word has always been such a metaphor. From Pope's rather delightful 'Rape of the Lock' in the eighteenth century to inane phrases that one uses unthinkingly – 'Feeling raped, man.' But if for the first time it's being taken seriously across the country, causing an uproar, if there are protests on the streets, if this is being seen as a watershed moment, I suppose it can't be a bad thing. I kept my temper in check even as I said this to Baba. I have no idea why some men feel more threatened with the idea of rape than women. Baba seems to think it is all a terrible fuss that needs to be nipped in the bud. I am here in Kolkata to meet my mother, to understand what is happening to her, not to discuss Nirbhaya, not to defend the girl who fought fiercely with her rapists to stay alive, whose spirit couldn't be broken. But I'm being maudlin.

Ma hovered around anxiously. Arguments make her nervous. She didn't quite know what we were arguing about but she was on my side. She always is, though she pretends to be neutral. It is this which cracks me up. Ma is easy to brainwash, but when it comes to me she will always be on my side. The burden of having a daughter in a family that doesn't respect women isn't easy for her. She didn't mind for herself – being superfluous – but she does mind when it comes to me.

I think of Alok. The oddness of having married him. How had I even done that? It was such a ridiculously lavish wedding too. Baba was delighted he had landed big fish; it had to be displayed and talked about. The proposal came because I was his daughter. Just like Ma went to fancy lunches because of him.

Anyway, poor Baba was only ticking certain boxes while I met Alok and his mother many times before the wedding. I should have noticed that something was weird there. Except that I did, and thought there was something wrong with me. Pre-bridal nerves and all that. I was uneasy but not enough.

Omar once said, 'I am glad Alok and his mother had sex or whatever. It meant that one day you and I would be together.' Ah well. That is one positive spin one can put on that!

I remember how tough Ma was when my marriage fell apart. The way she handled Alok and his parents with chilling condescension when they came to our house to beg me to return. She asked me to not come out of my room and she and Baba spoke to them. I could hear her voice, not loud but clear and strong. Divorce, paperwork, no thank you, please leave now – I can still recall clusters of words I overheard that day, more than twenty years ago.

I can remember the words and the young woman who heard them. It's difficult to recognize that woman as me. I can remember the woman who spoke the words too and it's almost impossible to recognize that woman as Ma. The almost-old woman who lacks coherence and with whom it is getting progressively more difficult to have a sensible conversation.

I wonder if Ma would have led a less fractured life if I hadn't been born. If Sudeep had been born first, they might not have had a second child. Ma doesn't really think outside of the personal. Let every woman on this planet be treated unfairly, she will say we deserve it as a species, we are inferior, but not her daughter.

I discuss this with Mashi, of whom Ma will always be suspicious. It is almost like she anticipates her displeasure and reacts to it, regardless of whether Mashi has expressed it or not. I suppose that happens between siblings and between partners. Between parents and children too. When you just know each other too well and know exactly what the other one is thinking without even exchanging a word. When I was in college I never told Ma how often I bunked classes, but when I came home in the evening I felt resentful. I didn't even tell her but her presence made me guilty. It was like she was my bloody conscience.

My grandfather told Ma and Mashi at the time of Ma's marriage that he chose a partner for Ma that he would never have chosen for Mashi. Why on earth would he say that? He set them up against each other with that comment. Ma has spent a lifetime defending her husband and in-laws to her sister.

'I thought Malini was overreacting at first and the results aren't conclusive yet, but still ...' I said to Mashi. Omar and I were visiting Mashi while Shazia was at home with Ma.

'It's difficult to tell with Didi. She has too many conflicting thoughts and yet she manages to present this very calm outward self,' Mashi said. Omar nodded.

'It's impossible to tell what she really thinks about anything – outside of what she knows she should think. What she has been taught to think,' Omar said. 'And she is far smarter than she lets on. But she doesn't like it when people don't get how intelligent she is. Quite a paradox is Ma.'

'I don't know. I never understood her insistence on being positive about everything. I saw it as wilful blindness, but perhaps that is unkind. She got married into a hugely conservative family which was so different from ours, where she had to cover her head every day in the presence of elders, touch a million relatives' feet every morning and practise all kinds of archaic rituals. Yet she managed to become the favourite daughter-in-law, sister-in-law, in that family,' Mashi said. 'I used to really wonder how she did it. That household was teeming with wives, sons, daughters and daughters-in-law – I couldn't bear most of them. But all of them loved Didi.'

I wasn't quite sure if I liked Mashi's description of my paternal family. I could sometimes understand why Ma would be defensive. If you know people intimately you also know their inner lives enough to appreciate who they are even if they are fundamentally different from you. What I loved best about Baba's family was the unselfconscious, merciless fun and humour that had never known political correctness. There was a charm in that which I can't explain. And the loudness and unapologetic pride in being who you are.

Ma didn't get that Mashi was also impressed with the way Ma had blended and triumphed in an alien setting. She just thought Mashi was mocking her all the time.

'But did Ma really start loving these people, her in-laws, or was it a duty she was fulfilling by making herself agreeable and liked?' Omar asked. He has always been intrigued with the way Ma navigates social relationships and pressures.

'It was a duty, I think. When Thakurda passed away I could tell she wasn't particularly moved. Even though the man had doted on her like crazy. The only reason I liked him was because he loved my mother. But she was discharging a duty and she had done it well. There was no sorrow attached to his death for her,' I said. 'I know I was a little appalled at her lack of emotion at his passing away.'

'When our father died though, Omar, she almost went into depression. Which I never saw coming. I always thought she cared less for him than I did somehow,' Mashi said. 'Anyway, Didi has always been full of surprises. I can never get her fully.'

I could though, I got my mother. But I had taken her for granted. I hadn't known that her mind, burdened under so many contradictions, would one day crack. I thought she knew how to live with them. If not harmoniously, at least with grace. Though if this is a genetic disorder all our dissections are moot. Her mind didn't crack, she was born with the errant gene or something like that.

Ma has told me many stories about the early years of her marriage. She was empathetic even towards those whom she couldn't identify with, in her trademark clinical way, and on many levels she enjoyed the bustle of a joint family, the colour, the chaos.

The younger generation in that large joint family went to Ma with all their secrets. One cousin of Baba's who was studying in IIT Kanpur wrote her long letters from his hostel – telling her about life on campus. His brother, another one of Baba's million cousins, had a girlfriend only Ma knew about. She belonged to a different caste so they never got married. Then there was Asim. He was closer to Baba's age – a couple of years older than Ma. He was very good-looking. He didn't talk much, was less communicative than the rest of the family. Ma's Asim story had always moved me somehow.

Ma had got into the habit of going to the terrace in the afternoons when she was a newlywed. Though she liked the joint family and all the chatter, she had been used to a different life at home. Quieter, less boisterous. The terrace gave her a little respite from the rest of the house. She had her own bedroom and living room in that mansion of a house but there was no concept of privacy. Everyone was here, there and everywhere.

The terrace was huge. It had to be, the house was so huge. On one end of the terrace there were two rooms. Like a hut. During the pujas, the crackers used to be stacked there. Piles and piles of chocolate bombs, rockets, kalipotka, tubri, chorkhi. I have faint memories of that too. Rest of the year, the rooms were empty. A thin coir mattress, a ceiling fan, a couple of pillows and a lamp were kept in one of the rooms – neat and clean. Ma had peeped in and wondered who used the room. The servants' quarters were downstairs. A small pile of books and some notebooks and pens were kept near the pillow.

One afternoon, Ma had been sitting on the terrace for about thirty minutes. She was feeling homesick, wondering if Mashi would have come home from school by then. They didn't have cell phones of course. To make a call from the telephone in the big living room one had to ask for permission. Her parents' house was only seven or eight kilometres away but she didn't have the permission to see or talk to her family as often as she would have liked.

So, she had been sitting on the terrace for half an hour or so when she heard some noise coming from one of the two rooms. The door was shut and the window too. Somehow, she didn't feel like inspecting but she also didn't feel like sitting there any more – it was a little uncomfortable, she didn't quite know why. As she made her way towards the steps leading downstairs, she heard the door opening and looked back to find Asim coming out of one of those rooms. With his friend. Ma had seen him with this friend many times. He stayed in the house next to theirs – the terraces were adjoined and the friend must have just crossed over to meet Asim. Usually Ma saw the two of them hanging out together on the street or in the room that Asim shared with his brothers.

After this day, Ma bumped into them on the terrace many times. Sometimes she knew they were in the room so she didn't disturb them. She didn't quite run away downstairs like she did the first time. And if they were outside the three of them would talk and Ma found Asim's friend intelligent and easy to talk to. She started looking forward to spending time with them. This continued for some years. Ma had been going to the terrace ever since I was born and she would take me up there in the afternoons to get some sun and air. Apparently Asim's friend really liked playing with me. I have no recollection of this person – I was less than a year old at that time. I know Asim kaka, of course, a quiet, nondescript man, with lovely manicured hands. But some months before Asim got married they stopped meeting on the terrace. His friend didn't even come for the wedding – everyone in the family commented on how rude that was. But his friend's mother said he had a high fever and couldn't get out of bed. I think that is what Ma told me. Though she guessed that Asim and he had fallen out and were not friends any more since Asim decided to get married.

I don't quite know why I narrated this story to Omar and Mashi now. Perhaps I wanted Mashi to know that Ma's life in the joint family hadn't lacked complexity. It wasn't only about touching everyone's feet in the morning. But I felt reluctant to discuss the story after narrating it. To take it apart, to break down the nuances. This is exactly how Ma had told me this particular story and I wanted it to stay this way.

'If it's a medical condition – dementia – then her personal history or how she lived her life doesn't really have anything to do with it, does it?' I said now, looking at Omar and Mashi for confirmation. 'A neurodegenerative disease. Not related to lifestyle or stress, would it be?'

I don't want it to be something that we could have avoided if we had been vigilant. I wanted it to be something that I couldn't have helped her with. That evening before dinner Omar spent a long time researching dementia. I couldn't get myself to do it.

Age is the most significant known risk factor for dementia. After the age of sixty-five, the risk of developing Alzheimer's disease doubles approximately every five years. It is estimated that dementia affects one in fourteen people over the age of sixty-five and one in six over the age of eighty.

Women are slightly more likely to develop Alzheimer's than men.

I don't know if Omar was choosing to read out the parts that would be most comforting for me though I wish he wouldn't keep saying Alzheimer's. I asked specifically and was told Ma doesn't have that.

'Why do you keep saying Alzheimer's, Omar? The doctor didn't say that. He said a form of dementia,' I said.

'Websites seem to use them interchangeably,' Omar said, absent-mindedly massaging my neck with his left hand while he continued to read what was on the screen. It felt good.

Ma and Shazia came into the room and Omar quickly closed the browser. Not that Ma would've tried to read over his shoulder. Come to think of it, Ma has never tried to sneak information out of me even when I was a teenager. She respects privacy or has been wise enough to know that she is better off not knowing everything in my life. Or it just could be that it never crossed her mind – she has always been a detached person in the nicest possible way. I feel the tears spring to my eyes and blink them away. It's going to be hard. We are still hoping it's reversible, something medicines can take care of.

Shazia came and sat on my lap. 'I beat Dimma in Chinese Checkers,' she said.

'Yes, she did,' Ma said happily. She hadn't been told what the doctor had said. As far as she is concerned, Malini is still the villain trying to prove she is ill for some unfathomable psychotic reason.

'Life doesn't suddenly become better after your mother-in-law's death,' Ma told me. 'I thought it would but it didn't. And Malini is so busy with her office, her laboratory work. How will she take over this household even if I'm ill or dying?'

Ma has been making these veiled accusations for a while now. About how materialistic and grasping Malini is, how her parents brainwash Sumeet into hating Baba and her. I mildly defend Malini but feel a little unsure. I assume there is at least a kernel of truth in what Ma says these days.

Yesterday Ma told me that she keeps losing money. She suspects Malini takes it. I couldn't pretend any more, even to myself. Ma is unwell. I didn't tell Omar what she said but one of the things he read out to me was that people with dementia sometimes imagine family members are stealing money from them or that the police are following them. Two common scenarios of delusional behaviour commonly referred to as paranoia, he said.

'I trust the staff,' said Ma. 'Sapna told me that Malini comes into my bedroom when I am out and rummages through the drawers and opens the cupboards. Why does she do it?'

'Maybe she was looking for something specific? Something she left in your room by mistake,' I replied. Sapna has been with our family for over twenty years. She loves Ma and hates Malini. She possibly noticed before all of us, before Malini, that Ma's mental state was fragile. I wouldn't put it past her to deliberately cause a rift between Ma and Malini. We now have to live with conflicting realities as far as Ma is concerned and never quite know which one is real and which is imagined.

I asked Sapna today how Ma was and she said Ma kept forgetting things, getting confused, buying the same groceries two or three times in a week.

'We are all getting old,' she added sagely. 'I work hard all day; I don't have the time to fall ill or forget things.'

I smiled. I wish it was that easy. If our memory and health failed only if we took time out for it. Like a boat ride on the Hooghly.

Ma's regular conversations are lucid and normal. She asks Omar about his parents, his brother and nephews. Occasionally she slips or says something strange like the time she asked Omar if his parents live in Cambridge. And then she shook herself out of it and said never mind, let's talk about something else. She does that while complaining about Malini sometimes, too. As if I was the one making silly accusations against her. She is otherwise a nice person, Ma will add, in Malini's defence!

I wonder how it will be. Watching a person I love slowly evaporate. I can only be happy that this didn't happen earlier. Time is the crux. A tragedy is defined by timing. To lose a leg when you are ten years old isn't the same thing as losing a leg when you are seventy. The sense of unfairness and loss won't be the same. The world is rampantly and insanely cruel and the point is not to pretend otherwise but to live on, with love and laughter and loss, in spite of it. I think of the Nirbhaya case being discussed relentlessly in the papers and on TV, every day, all the time. An iron rod being inserted into the vagina of a young girl. My insides recoil. Just open a newspaper if you want a perspective on justice and tragedy.

The personal–political and the political–personal. It seems that Ma is going down taking the nation with her. But that is rubbish. A=B and B=A are not that interchangeable. More like an analogy: A=B and C=D. Dementia is to Ma what fascism is to the right wing. Hypocrisy is to a politician (whatever wing!) what horns are to a rhinoceros.

Ma wants to stay with Omar and me. Not all the time, she reassured me, but a little more frequently than before. I know she told my cousin that she is happiest when she is with her daughter. All relationships are labelled now. My daughter. My son. My grandson. Almost as if she is holding on to the 'my' with all her might. A selfish appropriation where she places herself at the centre and fails to see the interconnections. Her daughter is also someone's sister is sometimes too much for her to comprehend. Straight one-on-one connections.

Ma no longer asks if I am tired when I return from a work appointment. Instead she tells me she is hungry or that she wants to take a bath. It's not a big deal, I know. But I can't help wonder where my mother went. My mother thought of me before she thought of herself. Always.

Ma is a practical consumer of news. When I am horrified by something in the papers she looks at me sympathetically as if the horror lies in her daughter having to cope with it rather than the news itself. She does worry that I am too soft. In August when she was visiting, Omar and I were discussing the Sikh temple attack that took place in Wisconsin that month. A tall, bald white gunman in his forties killed six people in the temple – domestic terrorism, hate crime, who knows what the reason was. Ma was listening to Omar and me talking about it.

'You are old enough to know these things happen – do you discuss such news every time there's something in the paper?' she asked us. It was a waste of time as far as she was concerned and a little naïve on our parts.

'Ma, what should we discuss then?' Omar said, amused. 'Only the things that don't happen?'

Ma giggled; she found Omar funny. 'You are right. But Sohini gets upset – it isn't good for her. She even cries when she watches a movie.'

'True, she is insane. Even Tom and Jerry makes her cry,' Omar said and Ma giggled again obligingly.

'As in, how silly, though it is way too violent – Tom and Jerry,' I said. 'But, Ma, if no one reacts to what happens in the world, how will things improve?'

'The world has been around for long enough without improving. Your getting bothered won't make any difference,' she said. 'And people are reacting – that is how you get to read what you read in the papers.'

Ma was all right with the rest of the world burning so long as the four or five people she cared for were fine. I have always found that frustrating, Ma's refusal to engage with the ways of the world. But there will come a time when

I will wish for that refusal to engage, it will be preferable to what she will be like some years from now as her brain cells continue to die. Even a refusal to engage is a show of agency. Will she still experience moments of lucidity and understanding when her dementia is more advanced? Or will she withdraw completely? Though a practical person in every other way, Ma has always been terrified of old age and what might come with it.

'Sudeep and you must let me go if I am unwell, don't try to keep me alive with surgery and medicines.' Ma has said this to me enough number of times for me to know she means it.

'Don't you want to live to see your grandchildren grow up?' I remember saying some thirty years back when she first told me she doesn't want to live to a grand old age.

'Why? How will that help?' Ma had replied, genuinely puzzled. The only thing that always terrified her was the idea of losing her own physical and mental faculties. Tough luck, Ma, I want to say now, with the same clinical practicality I have seen her practise. It is what you have to live with. Old age and a gradual lapse into the ridiculous. If Ma is told she has dementia she will willingly die today. She wouldn't want to live with hope, that wouldn't be the choice she would make. She isn't attached to the world the way most of us are. The wonders of the world don't tie her down; she has appreciated them and isn't curious about what comes next in this life. She would rather die with her dignity intact. But I don't think it's going to happen.

I wish I could spare her, the way she has always tried to spare me the horrors of the world, but I can't, just as she or anyone else for that matter can't spare me from what my future holds.

November 2015–February 2016

Mrs Chatterjee

In 1947, just after India won independence, Mahatma Gandhi came to Calcutta. My maternal grandfather, Dadu, was a lifelong admirer of Gandhi. He took me, his five-year-old granddaughter, with him to the grounds where Gandhi was addressing a crowd. We were lucky, we found a good place to stand and watch Gandhi as he spoke.

When we returned home Dadu said, 'I have seen Gandhi, I feel truly blessed. I am ready to die now.' He ate his lunch and went to his room to take a nap. He died in his sleep. I was five years old then but I remember it all clearly. How lucky my dadu was. He was a good man too.

My father died when he was seventy-three. I am seventy-three now. I am ready to die. Helping someone die isn't a bad thing. I wish someone would help me end my life, the way I helped my mother-in-law. Not that I helped her like that. I did get confused with the medicines sometimes. And she was so old, older than I am now. I don't know if she wanted to die like I do, even though she was bedridden and stuck in one room. Maybe those who are wicked like to live longer. The idea of dying and being unable to spread unhappiness must be sad for them. I would love to die. Not because I hate my life, but it really is time.

Or perhaps if my husband died it would be easier for me. He does have some of his mother's genes I know. He is constantly finding fault with me. He has taken away all the cupboard keys from me. He talks to the servants directly and discusses the day's menus with them. He gives me very little money to spend. He takes the accounts for ironing, groceries and everything else directly from the servants. He doesn't let me go out alone with the driver. He is punishing me but I don't know for what reason. He won't let me do anything. He calls me incompetent, spoilt and lazy. It makes me very sad. If one of us dies it would be good.

There is nothing wrong with dying. I won't mind if someone came with a knife and killed me. People can be cruel. They love killing. A man in a village called Dadri got killed for eating beef. He stole a cow from somewhere, cut it up and ate it. Obviously people would kill him for doing that. He was Muslim and the other people were Hindu. I don't eat cow because it is holy. I eat chickens and pigs because they aren't holy. Sanchita eats beef, she even cooks it in her house. Once she served beef at a party. Thankfully my husband and I were not invited. This was many years back when the children were small. I do not think my husband would have gone to such a party where beef was being served. Not in India, he would not. I think Sanchita likes to shock and annoy him. She always has.

I don't know if Omar eats beef. In any case, he is not a poor, helpless Muslim man. He comes from a cultured background. Even if he ate beef people would not mind. It's cheap meat, beef, and unclean. I do hope Omar and his family don't eat it.

My husband told me about the man in Dadri who ate beef. While we were having breakfast. He was reading the newspaper. 'We Hindus are tolerant but there are limits,' he said. I nodded.

The next morning at breakfast he said, not looking up from the newspaper, 'Now they are saying it wasn't beef in the fridge, it might have been mutton.'

I was upset. 'We never eat beef. Who put it in the fridge? It will have to be cleaned now.'

My husband laughed in a rather mean way and said something under his breath before speaking to me. 'I told you about a man who got lynched to death by Hindus in his village for keeping beef in the fridge. Remember? A Muslim man, Mohammed something?'

I did remember and it worried me. 'I hope Omar does not do such things. He is such a nice boy. He won't, I think. Should we phone him and tell him to be careful?'

'Yes, you must do that. I have to go now.' He got up, folding the newspaper and sighing, I do not know why. 'Sapna, come and take your Boudi upstairs.'

I don't need help to go upstairs, but he has been behaving like this all the time. He wants people to believe

I cannot do anything myself. Once I went for a walk in the neighbourhood park and got a little lost. Once in a mall too. My husband will keep reminding me of that and try to scare me into not going out. Malls are confusing places. Everything looks the same in a mall. I got disoriented. Anyone can get lost in a mall. I sat down on a bench and phoned Sohini in Delhi.

'What do you see near you?' Sohini asked me. I told her the names of the shops nearby.

'Stay where you are,' she said. 'I will tell the driver to come and get you.'

Sohini phoned the driver. He came and got me from the bench and took me home. It was not a problem really but my husband got to know and banned me from going out alone any more. This was some time back. Now I do not even have money. I cannot go to a mall and get lost or buy things even if I want to.

When I got lost in the park one lady who I asked for directions lent me her phone to call my husband. But I could not remember his number. She was very kind and took me to her house to have tea. She lived next to the park. So I did. Then she offered to take me to the police station but as we went across the park I met Malini. I introduced her to the lady.

'We have been frantic for the last two hours,' said Malini, thanking the lady profusely. The lady told Malini that I had asked for directions but couldn't remember the house number. Once we were alone, Malini turned to me and said, 'You must not go out alone like that.'

'I think the lady was happy I was lost. She seemed lonely. She got a chance to help someone. I suppose it can be nice to help a lost person. She must have felt noble and good,' I said to Malini.

'And now you are mocking someone who went out of her way to help you …' Malini said. She looked unhappy. I did not mean to mock anyone. Malini obviously wanted me to feel bad.

My husband and Malini are best friends now. There was a time when they could not stand each other. Now they put their heads together and come up with ways to stop me from going out and enjoying life.

Luckily, I found money wrapped up in a sari that I was going to wear. I took the money and went out with Sapna and the driver. I bought six saris that day. I still socialize and go to parties after all. Though the last time I went for lunch I was a little embarrassed.

'It is so sweet the way you wear the same sari all the time,' Mridula had said.

'I don't really care about appearances,' I told her.

'I know. I like that about you,' she said. But I knew she did not mean it.

Malini got to know that I had gone sari shopping. She tracks my movements like a secret agent. God only knows why.

'What did you buy, Ma?' she asked politely enough. I knew she had scolded the driver and Sapna for taking me out without her permission. As if she is the boss of us all.

'Some saris. I wear the same sari to every party. I needed some new ones,' I said.

'Ma, you have plenty of saris. Of course you can buy new ones if you like, but you definitely have many in your cupboard,' she said. It seems she really does go through my cupboards when I'm not around, otherwise how would she know that? 'You must have had a lot of money on you if you bought so many saris.'

My husband used to give me unlimited amounts of money. I would hide it away in the folds of saris or in old biscuit tins. Who is Malini to ask me crude questions of this sort? She is a bad, greedy person. Unfortunately, she is married to my son and I have to put up with her.

One day I went upstairs in the evening and found Malini coming out of my bathroom. I found that the towels were on the floor and there was no soap in the soap dish. There was water everywhere and the whole bathroom was a mess. I don't know what Malini had been up to. I called Sapna. She came, shaking her head. She cleaned up without complaining. Sapna is a good person.

I contemplate different ways of dying. Hanging should be easy. Just put a rope around the neck and hang from the fan. Though where would I get a big, strong rope? Maybe a sheet would do. I imagine entering my bedroom and finding my husband hanging from the fan. I would scream and call Sapna. But I do not think he wants to kill himself. He knows all about hanging. I was very worried when he got into a fight with Sohini and Omar about hanging. They all got so angry.

Afzal Guru, Yakub Memon. Judicial hangings. All kinds of angry names and words. I don't like my husband to fight with Sohini. I just looked straight at the wall across the room to calm myself. There is a thangka on that wall that we got from Tibet many years ago. It looks crooked. I must straighten it.

'I like our thangka,' I said to them. 'It's a wall hanging. But judicial hangings are surely different.'

I was joking of course, but none of them laughed. Omar put an arm around my shoulders and said, 'Very different, Ma, but your thangka is nicer.'

I was glad that they stopped arguing after that. Sohini was about to speak again when Omar shook his head at her. Such a sensible boy.

'I saw Mahatma Gandhi with my grandfather when I was a child,' I said to change the topic for them. 'India had just become independent. I am only a little older than India.'

'And wiser possibly,' said Omar. That was sweet of him. I don't know if I am really wise but I am glad he thinks so.

'It might be fashionable to be dismissive of your own nation but it doesn't serve any purpose,' my husband said.

'Is it better to pretend everything is hunky-dory even if it isn't?' Sohini said, looking at her father. 'Sometimes medicines are needed. They have to be given.'

I felt bad. I knew she was talking about me now. She was angry with her father for not supervising my medicines. I knew that, Sapna had told me.

'I take the medicines when I feel like. Sometimes Admenta, sometimes this other one,' I had laughingly told

Sohini but she was not amused. 'I am fine, Sohini, really. It is all rubbish.'

I do not want to take the medicines. My husband and I believe that one should not take medicines as far as possible. Sohini and Sudeep were hardly ever medicated as children. But Malini has brainwashed all of them into believing I need medicines. If Sohini gives me the medicines, or Sudeep, I have them. But when my husband or Malini hands them to me I stick them under my tongue and spit them out later. I am supposed to have medicines twice a day. Whenever Sohini is with me she will make sure I am following the prescriptions. To make her happy I take the medicines when she is around.

When my husband and I are alone he does not bother. Some days he will suddenly remember and ask me if I am taking my medicines. I tell him I do not need them. He says the children get upset when I do not have my medicines properly. He makes Sapna get the box and sorts the medicines out for me. Truth is, I do not trust him too much any more. I don't mind taking the medicines if they will help me die but I feel they are meant to make me go mad, which I do not want.

I visit a psychologist once a week. I did not want to go when Malini first broached the idea, but Sohini explained to me that it was just like that, for no particular reason. Everyone goes to psychologists these days, to chat and unburden. The psychologist is a sweet young girl. I tell her many things.

I talk to her about my father and mother. My father was a great man but he came from an impoverished family. A self-made man. My mother used to drive a car which was very uncommon for girls in those days and she played tennis. They had tennis courts in their house. Yet she fell in love with my father. He was charismatic and intelligent. When my mother's family worried about how she would live without the luxuries she had grown up with, my Baba vowed to himself that he would be a very rich and influential man one day. He worked towards that and became a name to reckon with in Calcutta in the 1940s and for the rest of his life. I like ambitious, successful men. Women, on the other hand, should be good and kind. Sohini might argue with me but these are simple truths. I would not have had a happy life if my father or husband had been mediocre men.

I could see the psychologist girl was impressed. She comes from a middle-class family. Her father worked hard to educate her. He had a government job and taught kids in the evenings. Poor man, the combination of sharpness and IQ that results in an exceptional person is not common, though I have been fortunate enough to be associated with many such men, from my father to my husband. Her family is very proud of her, she told me once. I want to help her improve herself. For instance, she could wear clothes that are less middle class. The colours hurt my eyes and that synthetic fabric could not be comfortable either. It is good her parents have brought her up well despite all the hardships they had to undergo but you cannot go very far if you do not learn how to dress and carry yourself well.

My husband's family has had money for many generations. They are proud of their family name and make fun of new money. My in-laws would pass comments about my parents that were difficult for me to swallow without retorting.

'I wonder how Sudha's family let her marry your father – it was the talk of Calcutta in those days. It affected her sisters' marriage prospects too,' my father-in-law told me; Sudha was my mother's name. I wanted to ask him why he had married his son to such a man's daughter. Just because he was rich and powerful? My father had a brilliant mind; my own dadu, my mother's father, recognized that when he allowed Ma to marry him. Dadu was a gentleman, soft and good, but he could recognize talent when he saw it. Everyone else in my mother's family was horrified when she declared she was going to marry Baba, except her father. My dadu said my father was a fine man and he was going to do well for himself.

My grandmother threatened to commit suicide when my mother said she was marrying Baba. She was rather annoying. I never liked visiting my grandparents because I knew the day would end with Ma fighting with her mother for some reason or the other. Theirs was a beautiful house, all marble and open spaces and curved staircases and rooms and rooms full of curios, antiques, and heavy, elaborately carved, dark wooden furniture. Yet I was never comfortable there. I would keep pulling my mother's sari and asking her when we could go home. That would make my grandmother angry.

'You want to go home to that hole in the wall you live in?' she would say to me rudely and I would defiantly reply yes. My father was on his way to success but we still lived as a joint family with his sisters and brother. We were all packed into the small house like sardines. But my mother made sure our room was neat and tidy. My father had constructed a good tiled bathroom just for my mother when they got married. He knew that she would find it difficult to use the dingy toilet that the rest of his family shared. He was always thoughtful that way. As far as possible he made life easier for my mother and he was aware that growing up she had been used to better.

We moved into our own house the year I turned ten and Sanchita was just two. After living in a joint family, with so many cousins and uncles and aunts, I was not very happy to be alone with my parents and sister. I think Baba and I were always a little sad about leaving the old life and family behind. Ma was happy and Sanchita was too young to remember the joint family. She was born after Baba became rich, she did not remember the early years of struggle, of our parents arguing about money in lowered voices, the way I did.

'I hope you are not getting bored?' I said to the psychologist girl. I loved meeting her every week and talking about the past. I think she was very fascinated by my stories. She was not used to success stories like I was.

'Oh, not at all. It is all so interesting,' she said. 'And how are your husband and family?'

I did not really want to tell her. It is not correct to talk about domestic problems with outsiders, though Sohini told me I should talk to the psychologist freely. How to tell her that my husband is not a very nice man? He has the same cruel streak that his mother had. But it is all right for men to not be nice. They have so many responsibilities, they know how the world works and about the bad things that go on. Nice men finish last. My mother-in-law just sat at home, not reading the newspapers but pronouncing judgements on everything. Her son is better than that.

'My husband wants me to read newspapers,' I told the psychologist. 'To understand the world better.'

'That is excellent,' she exclaimed. 'You should read the papers; you could even make clippings of the events that are of interest to you and put them in a scrapbook.'

'Yes, the refugees. Muslim refugees. I will make a scrapbook,' I said.

'Just the Muslim refugees?' The psychologist laughed, and I felt a little insulted.

'My son-in-law is a Muslim. My husband likes him, but not other Muslims. And my husband is angry with the way refugees are going here and there, all over the world, trying to take over,' I said.

'Oh, is that so? I didn't know your son-in-law is Muslim.' She seemed very interested in learning more about Omar but I did not want to tell her. It is better not to talk about family matters.

'He is not a refugee,' I said shortly. 'He comes from a cultured family.'

'I am sure,' she said, trying to be nice. 'Where did your daughter meet him?'

'Not in Syria,' I said. My husband keeps talking about Syria and the crisis there. This psychologist might think Omar is from Syria. 'I will make the scrapbook and show my husband. Thank you for the idea. Maybe it will make him less angry with me.'

'He is angry with you?' She looked concerned. I did not want to tell her about how he shouted at me, accused me of misplacing his shoes, clothes, everything, of ruining his life by being an ignorant sort of person. 'But he looks after you so well, he came and met me and talked about you.'

'That is good,' I said. I do not know why he would have talked about me though. With this girl he hardly knows. I do not talk about him with anyone if I can help it. I got up to leave.

'I will meet you again next week. In the meantime, try to finish that painting you told me you started. And don't miss your yoga classes,' she said cheerfully. It is her job to sound cheerful.

I nodded. Sometimes she spoke to me as if I was a little child, but I do not mind. She is a good girl. It is lonely at home with no one to talk to. I like coming here and talking to her.

Sohini

A distorted version of the person remains. The goodness that was Ma is now reduced to tiresome dithering. Much of her is just a mass of petty paranoia. The IQ reduced to next to nothing yet she knows she was not this person before and tries to compensate with senseless comments that attempt to captivate. It is hard to watch. The person who was the backbone of my life even as recently as four or five years back. The dying brain cells have ravaged her. Even when I see her shuffling around now, I see the person that was, I see the woman who did her best for her children and was fiercely protective of them, who lived in her own world yet was practical and impatient and busy.

I don't know if Ma is grappling with the disease with some awareness of what she is doing, if she realizes how much she has changed. When she forgot my birthday for the first time three years back she was confused and apologetic. Ma knew better than anyone else how much I loved my birthday. When she wanted to distract me as a child she would start planning my party, even if it was eight months away. She organized a surprise party for my fortieth with Omar. The person who did that is gone, leaving behind a lady who asks if it is morning or night at 11 a.m. Who sits down for breakfast and asks if we are going to have lunch or dinner. She isn't self-conscious about it any more. Even a year back it used to bother her that she was forgetting and she would try to come up with excuses. Now she is unapologetic.

'There was a person under my bed last night. It was a little disturbing. He kept saying, "Mrs C, Mrs C,"' Ma told me recently.

'Could you have dreamt that?' I asked her.

'I suppose. Possible,' she said agreeably. Her basic framework hasn't disintegrated. She is still an unassuming person who likes to please, strives to be happy.

I try to remember the efficient person who took care of the running of a huge household, who spent lavishly, who knew exactly where things were kept. If I couldn't find something I knew she would find it for me. I remember waiting for her to come back from a wedding when I couldn't find my History textbook and needed it desperately for a test in school the next day. I suspected she had a magic wand, the way she could find just about anything that I had misplaced. If Omar asks me to get something from the market I will likely forget, for two days at least, and possibly remember on the third. Or he will get it himself without reminding me again. But with Ma we would just have to mention in passing that the toothpaste was running out in the bathroom and a new one would be there at night.

It angered me at first. I blamed her for succumbing to a disease. Strong people fight back. Only the weak succumb. Though the fact remains that strong people die for the same reasons as the weak. Forget about strong people, children die. Children die from illness, from accidents, from bullets. When terrorists systematically killed roomfuls of children in the Army Public School in Peshawar a year ago, I felt it was the death of humanity. Which is stupid. Humanity has been dead forever. The photographs of those beautiful children, rosy-cheeked and smiling, did something to me. The children of Peshawar were exceptionally beautiful which lent a certain aesthetic to their death. My mother put that idea into my head.

Ma was less muddled then than she is today and watched the news on TV diligently. She still does but with no knowledge of what she is watching.

'Some very good-looking children died in Pakistan,' she told me then. 'In Bengal, our children aren't so beautiful – you know, when I was born I was very dark and my grandmother said I looked like a rat. I felt sad seeing how beautiful these children were.'

Ma has always lacked political correctness in a guileless way that is almost deliberate. It isn't that she is stupid. I think she used superficiality as a weapon sometimes – to fight fire with fire.

We still try to see Ma as a continuation of the person she was. Sometimes it works, sometimes it doesn't. I blame

Baba, unfairly perhaps. Her mind might have cracked because of how he always treated her. A step out of line and he would pull her back. The only way she could have defied his authority was by losing her mind and that is precisely what she has gone and done. The ultimate subversion.

Would Ma not have had dementia if she had had a softer partner? That isn't something we will ever know. If a stray gene was waiting patiently to manifest itself till she was seventy, would a mere difference in lifestyle or attitudes have shut that gene up? Ma had an uncle, her Phoolkaka, who was a source of entertainment for us. I wonder if what we passed off as his eccentricity might not have been undiagnosed dementia.

When I was in my late teens Ma received an inland letter from her Phoolkaka. In those days, sky blue inland forms were used for writing letters to friends and family far away. For those outside the country we used aerogrammes which were slightly longer, a concession perhaps for the fact that they would have to travel further. Inland letters and aerogrammes had to be folded along the red dotted lines and sealed and sent off with the sender's address at the back.

When I wrote to my cousins I used to make my handwriting small and cram in as much as possible into each letter to make it worth the money and effort. It would reach them at the whimsy of the post office staff. Sometimes after two days, sometimes after a week. But they did reach.

Phoolkaka's inland letter to Ma didn't care to utilize the space provided. He had typed two lines which made us laugh and laugh.

Dear Anita,

Please send me four wheels. I have an Ambassador car but no wheels.

Thanking you in advance.

Yours,

Phoolkaka

The rest of the paper remained empty. Just the two sentences floating like kites in a clear blue sky. Using a typewriter instead of a pen was strange in itself, but we were cruel enough to be amused rather than bewildered by the idea of this old man sitting at his typewriter and writing strange words that made sense only to himself.

Towards the end of his life Phoolkaka was bedridden, he had to be fed intravenously through translucent pipes. His wife who was batshit crazy told Ma and Mashi when they went to visit him that she was stuffing chicken stew and all his favourite food into the pipes.

'It will be so boring for him otherwise,' she said. Mashi told me she was appalled but they knew Phoolkakima better than to contradict her. And, of course, we were all much entertained. It isn't mean to laugh at the strange ways of other people. They laugh at our strangeness, too, surely. It all evens out in the end.

After he died my parents went to visit his family. Phoolkakima was full of delightful stories again.

'We had such fun at the shoshan ghat,' Phoolkakima said. She had just returned from the cremation. In those days only men went to the shoshan ghat, but no one would have dared to stop Phoolkakima. 'My daughter-in-law and I swam across the Hooghly – just like that. Back and forth, from one bank to another, not just once but twice.'

Phoolkaka was very fond of Ma when she was a child. In the days when they still lived in a joint family and the house was teeming with relatives. He used to drop Ma to school and check her homework every evening. Ma was a diligent child and Phoolkaka showed the neat pages of her notebooks to the other children in the house as examples of how hard-working and intelligent Ma was.

Ma told me stories from their joint family days after Phoolkaka passed away. She didn't seem particularly perturbed by his death but it did make her nostalgic. Phoolkaka was the kindest person Ma had ever known. She felt sure Phoolkaka wouldn't have minded that we laughed at the inland letter he sent. But he wouldn't have laughed himself. If he was alive and knew about Ma today he would have been upset and anxious, not amused.

I went to meet Ma's psychologist in Kolkata. Malini had met her already and said she was crap. I had hoped to disagree with her. Baba had selected the psychologist. It would have made me feel better to know that Ma was in good hands. I sat through one of Ma's sessions with her.

'She talks about you a lot. I know everything about you and your husband.' The psychologist was younger than I expected and seemed pleased to meet me. She asked Ma what she had been doing to keep herself busy that week and cheered her on with platitudes. *Very good, Mashima. No, no, that is enough, don't worry. Whatever makes you happy, do that.*

'Your mother has had such an interesting life,' she told me. Ma looked pleased. I suppose if these sessions made her happy there was no harm in them. Ma has lost her conversational skills. Untethered words float here and there in half-sentences. None of her friends made any particular efforts to understand what she said any more. I don't know if she sought understanding either. She seemed to meander and muddle her way around words without any real attempt to communicate. She was lucid when she spoke about the past. It was the last ten or even twenty years that she had a problem with. And especially the 'now'. She had a confused sense of the passing days with no grip on dates, people she met when she went out or what was actually happening around her. The day after I leave Calcutta she might call and say it's been so long since I visited and that she's dying to meet me.

Sudeep and I want Ma to be who she was before she had dementia. We hoped for a reversal of the symptoms. It wasn't going to happen but still we hoped like the children we once were, who believed their mother could do wonders and set the world right. When Sudeep at age four had spilled milk on the floor and denied it, Ma said she knew it was him because she had special eyes that were trained on him from wherever in the world she might be.

'Ma, are you a god?' Sudeep had asked reverently. I was six and more sceptical but I too waited for Ma's reply with curiosity.

'No, but mothers have special powers too,' she had replied.

I have been turning more and more to Mashi in the last three or four years. I always thought of Ma and her as very different people. Yet, as Ma fades, I find myself clinging to my aunt. They have the same voice and intonation when talking, the same smile and walk, the same quick way of dealing with problems. I tell Mashi about my work, my life, the way I used to tell Ma about it all. I feel a need to fill the gap that Ma's absence has created. I wonder if it's disloyal to seek substitutes or if it's the only practical method of dealing with pain. Mourning those who aren't dead comes with peculiar baggage.

I talk to Ammi and Abba more, too. Especially about Shazia. They dote on Shazia while my Baba has a tough time remembering her name. And he isn't even the one with dementia. Baba likes Omar though – I am pretty sure of that. He is that very common sort of person in the world today. An Islamophobe who makes exceptions for the Muslims in his life but condemns those he doesn't know. Baba has scaled up his act in the last few years. He acrimoniously attacks everything Islam. Perhaps also to prove that in spite of having a Muslim son-in-law he impartially has reservations about the community.

'Mind you, it was Jinnah who proposed the two-nation theory,' Baba told me when I was visiting Calcutta without Omar last year. He said it as if I held him personally responsible for the creation of Pakistan.

I nodded. Since I didn't reply, he continued, 'Hindus constituted 27 per cent of Pakistan's population at the time of Partition; now there's just 3 or 4 per cent. They have been systematically decimated.'

'Forty thousand Muslims have been killed in the last few decades too. In Pakistan.' I wasn't sure if the figure I quoted was correct. But thereabouts for sure.

'How does that matter to me? Let them kill each other if they want. I only want them to leave my people alone,' Baba said. I thought of the Army Public School children in Peshawar. It did matter to me. Not the religion but the senselessness of violence.

'My husband and daughter are Muslim so I can't say they can kill each other like you just did.' I tried to smile. I hated getting personal in an argument but I wanted him to realize that whether he liked it or not they were his people by extension too. Empathy is not very easy to come by. For a lot of people, it only hurts when it gets personal. It must be nice for them – insensitive people are definitely more self-satisfied than others. Unfortunate for the rest of the world.

Baba looked a little uncomfortable but he didn't agree with me. The world is too polarized now for us to even grant each other a little grace.

I try not to argue with Baba when Ma is around. It distresses her. I have tried to tell her (in the past) that I don't find Baba's comments hurtful, just annoying and moronic. But that isn't true and she knows it as well as I do. She still does. It is one thing she is aware of even as so many of her thoughts and memories fade into nothingness. She remembers her childhood clearly but after her teen years are done, the memories shining and intact till then, she starts getting confused, her memory inversely proportionate to every subsequent year after that. Till what she did five minutes back is what she finds the toughest to remember.

It is a well-charted linear path along which Ma's mind walks. The ruthlessness with which her brain cells are dying is not random; there is a pattern to it. There is always a pattern to destruction and even while we see the grid, we are dumbstruck before it. A systematic, progressive meaninglessness which is difficult to counter.

Baba is Enemy No. 1 for Ma now. The years and years of serving him have coalesced into this hatred. Where Baba is concerned, Ma has never been ambivalent. It was always love or hate; she can't see him as an ordinary person, he inspires only extreme responses from her. I know she loved him though, for many, many years. She wasn't faking it. But her thoughts were always wrapped in binaries; she negated herself in order to keep him firmly on a pedestal.

He sometimes gets tired of me which is understandable; I am not good enough for him.

He knows exactly what is right and what is wrong; I don't know how to judge these things.

I know he loves me even though he is far smarter and better-looking than me.

I am so lucky to have got him though I don't know what he got in return.

I suppose it couldn't go on forever. Her love was deep, bolstered by conditioning and unthinking adulation. Ma wanted to feel lucky, wanted to believe that she of all the women she knew had landed the jackpot. Even though she might not be the smartest and most beautiful. It was a warped inverse pride and love that unfortunately couldn't last till the end of her life.

She had placed poor Baba right up there next to God (to be noted that Ma is a closet atheist, I read the signs). I remember how dutifully she would do the alpona in the puja room before all those auspicious pujas that were observed in our house.

'Do you enjoy doing this?' I was sitting next to her and admiring her deft strokes and the intricate designs she wove with rice paste.

'Yes, it's like doing a painting,' she replied.

'A special painting for God,' I said. I was ten or eleven years then and quite devout.

'Never thought of it like that,' Ma said, almost smirking. I was a little hurt.

'Why not?'

'I am sure God doesn't have time for all this – these are things we do to keep ourselves happy,' she shrugged.

Okay, so she had elevated Baba to a pedestal right next to the God she didn't quite believe in. So when he came crashing down, it was dirty. He was rolling in the mud and she wanted to stamp on him, obliterate him for good.

'But you are trying to understand with logic what is a mind diagnosed with dementia,' Omar said to me.

'Yes, but surely there has to be some logic, some pattern that every mind follows, even when the person isn't in full possession of every faculty,' I said. 'Every person with dementia won't be reacting in the same way to every stimulus; it will depend on some core qualities the person always possessed.'

'I suppose.' Omar frowned. 'Everyone won't react in the same way … but maybe the reactions are random. There will be a link to who you were but it might be more tenuous than you are thinking.'

I discussed Ma with Omar and with Mashi on the phone often. It was bloody depressing otherwise. I cracked jokes at Ma's expense because I would be lost without humour. Taking potshots at her made me feel that she had agency; she was not just a poor old woman who deserved pity and charity.

Ma might call me twice in ten minutes and repeat herself verbatim – all animated and excited.

'I want to go to America and visit my cousin sisters for a few weeks. I will stay at your house and visit them during the day,' she said yesterday.

Even six months back I might have tried to tell her that America isn't in Delhi. Now I just say, 'Okay, Ma, we can plan that.'

After five minutes she called again and said the exact same thing as if she was saying it for the first time. And again I said, yes, we can plan that.

At some level I prefer this. Earlier she was hesitant, she would have a dim sense of making a fool of herself in some way. Now she is confident and energetic.

I heard from a cousin that Ma is the laughing stock of Kolkata society. Her behaviour is sweet and embarrassing. Apparently she made quite a spectacle of herself at a school reunion she attended recently. When the school anthem was being played (and the alumni members getting all emotional) she started skipping around, clapping and singing along. She must have been pleased because she remembered the song. 'To East and West of that fair isle ...' – childhood memories delight her. My cousin said some people were annoyed because it was supposed to be a solemn moment. The singing of the school anthem is sacrosanct and the disturbing of it by a person with dementia can be irritating. For the rest of the world. Not for me. This person is my mother, so not for me.

Debolina and Arindam visit Ma every time she is in Delhi. She likes that because she remembers Arindam. Friends I introduce her to now disappear into the black hole of her mind, but Arindam was my friend in college. I don't hyperventilate about Omar and Debolina any more. It would be a waste of time. There is a lingering infatuation but neither of them will act on it. It's a safe sort of infatuation. Then, Arindam and Debolina's eleven-year-old son has a crush on Shazia who is all of nine now. Omar urges Shazia to be nice to him and Debolina gushes about how Riday brushes his hair twenty times before meeting

Shazia. So we have these intergenerational romances playing out. There is not enough love in the world in any case. Let me not object to the diverse manifestations of it! Jokes apart, they are family now. They are the closest couple friend we have and Arindam has always been important to me.

My worst fear is of the day when I will walk into the room and Ma will not recognize me. Though it will possibly happen sooner than later and then I won't have to be scared any more. The ultimate revenge of the Alzheimer's patient. Reduce every relative's and friend's sense of importance by forgetting. Not anger, not love, just don't know who you are and really don't care. I still hold on to the thought that Sudeep and I are indispensable to her sense of well-being. But we will be forgotten too. By the person who loved us the most.

Mrs Chatterjee

I am sitting in Omar and Sohini's living room while they are talking. They go on and on. Someone is in jail. A president.

'Is it Zail Singh?' I ask them. The Sikhs want Khalistan. Maybe that is why someone put Zail Singh in jail.

'No, Ma,' says Omar. 'The President of the JNU Students' Union. He's a student himself. Not anyone that you know of.'

I am glad to hear that. At the time of India's independence everyone was proud to go to jail. Nehru, Gandhi, Patel, everyone. But now the jails are full of other types of people, maybe murderers or thieves. It isn't prestigious to go to jail. But Sohini sounds worried. She says something about sedation.

'Was the person sedated in jail?' I ask. That is worrying. Sedatives are used in hospitals. If I am sedated and taken to jail it will be absurd.

'Sedated?' Omar sounds confused. 'No, I don't think so. Why, Ma?'

'I said "sedition".'

Sohini exchanges a knowing look with Omar. I don't like it when they do that. I know what sedition means but can't remember right away. I don't want to ask.

'Why has this student been put in jail if you don't mind my asking?' I ask politely.

'He apparently raised anti-national slogans but that isn't really true,' Sohini says.

'Anti-national? Haven't the British left?' It is confusing. I thought they left when I was a child.

'Yes, they left. The students were asking for freedom from inequalities, from injustices, equality for women, and so on,' Omar says. 'So it isn't right to put him in jail.'

'If he didn't do anything wrong they will leave him, don't worry.' Omar and Sohini should not get excited about every person in prison who must have done something bad.

'The student is from the university I went to, Ma – JNU,' Omar says.

'Cambridge?' I ask.

'No, this was before I went to England. I have told you before. This is where I got my master's degree.'

'Oh, that place where they have revolution?' I remember my husband saying this now and then about Omar's university.

'Yes, Ma.' Sohini is laughing. 'Good revolutions though. For change, for the underprivileged in our country.'

I wish Sohini wouldn't keep saying these things. Our country is doing so well. It has so many rich people now.

Even maids have mobile phones and refuse to work for anything less than five thousand rupees, or is it fifty thousand?

Omar had gone to his study. Now he comes back and says that he is going out and will be back in a few hours.

'Where are you going?' I ask. I wouldn't mind going out myself. 'Can I come with you and sit in the car and wait for you?'

'I am going to JNU, Ma, for a protest march. We can go out later in the night if you are tired of sitting at home.'

'Protest march?' I feel worried again. 'You have everything that you want. Aren't you happy? Why are you protesting?'

'I will tell you when I come back. Or Sohini will explain it to you.'

And then he is gone. I like Omar very much. He should be more careful. They have a child together. I forget the child's name, but if something happens to Omar it will be difficult for the child. Shazia. I remember now. She is my granddaughter. Very pretty girl. It will be easy for her to find a husband.

'Your father won't like this,' I tell Sohini now that she has started talking about students and politics again. I'm hoping that since he is a man she will take him more seriously than me.

'There is no virtue in unthinking patriotism. I don't see why he should mind,' Sohini says.

'Protesting isn't good. You do your work. Let others do their work. Stay safe,' I reply.

'As a Muslim in this country today I don't think Omar feels wonderfully safe,' Sohini tells me.

I am shocked. I don't know why they feel this way. There were Muslim girls in my class who didn't feel that way. Shabana, Naseem and Zara. Such nice girls, though Shabana came to school in a burkha which she took off after entering the school gates. Her family was a little extreme. Naseem's mother made the best biriyani. With mutton, of course; they did not use beef.

I don't know why Omar should not feel safe. If my husband hears this kind of talk he will be really angry. It is us Hindus who should be scared now, he says, because of the way the Muslims are sitting on our heads. It is just his way of talking. The Muslims don't really sit on anyone's heads. That would be funny. But my husband will be angry with Omar. I need to protect Omar because he is a good boy.

'Tell Omar to be careful. I don't want your father to get angry with him,' I say to Sohini.

'I don't think I care. Baba is such a hypocrite,' Sohini says and I feel alarmed. My husband is a very powerful person in Calcutta. He can make life difficult for anyone if he wants to. Like me. He got angry with me the other day because I cut up his white kurta to use as toilet paper since there was none in the bathroom. He went on and on scolding me till I got really scared.

'You could have used water, no, Ma?' Sohini said when I told her how angry he got with me.

'I needed toilet paper,' I said. 'I thought he will kill me. So angry he was.'

'Don't worry. He won't do anything,' Sohini said, but how do I tell her that I do not feel worried for myself so much as for Omar. Suppose he tries to kill Omar? Omar is Sohini's husband, so I must not tell her about my suspicions. I do not want her to get scared. I will just have to protect Sohini and Omar in my own way. When I return to Calcutta, I must take matters into my own hands.

When Omar comes back at night – or is it morning – he is tired but excited. He tells us about the human chain formation which I do not fully comprehend. To make chains out of human beings would involve killing so it cannot be that. My husband never goes for human chain formations. If he did maybe he wouldn't return and I wouldn't have to worry about Omar.

Then Omar says that his name is on a list of students who have been charged with sedition. Sedition, not sedation. For which people are put in jail. I am astounded at how he is sitting calmly and saying all this.

'Omar, is this true? What should we do?' I cut into their conversation because I am too worried.

'What is true, Ma?' he asks.

'You have to go to jail for sedating?' I am getting confused again, but I am too agitated to think straight.

'Why should he go to jail?' Sohini asks me.

'I heard what he said,' I tell her. I do not like it when people pretend they never said something that they did say. 'His name is on a list of people who have to go to jail.'

'Oh no, Ma, not this Omar.' Omar and Sohini are both smiling. 'It's another Omar. Umar, in fact. Umar Khalid. A student leader on the campus.'

I don't believe her. They obviously don't want me to worry but it is too late. I *am* worried.

'We don't know Umar personally but we believe he is a good boy, and, inshallah, nothing is going to happen to him,' Omar says and I see Sohini's eyes well up.

'Why are you crying if you don't even know him?' I ask Sohini.

'I am not crying, you know I get emotional easily like a fool,' she says. This is true, but this time I do not think she is getting emotional for no reason. She is trying to cover up because Omar will go to jail. And then her father will be so angry. But it is also true that Sohini gets emotional easily. When she was small she was a very sensitive child. Once when she was two years old, a snake entered our house in Shantiniketan. One of the servants picked up a stick and ran to kill it. Sohini screamed at him to stop, to not harm the snake. She was a little girl but she ran forward and held his arm, not scared of the snake at all. I yelled and scooped her up.

'Don't hit the snake, it will get hurt,' she kept saying. 'Its mother will cry.'

'You come away with me, Sohini, and let Haridada take the snake back to its mother,' I said. I took her into our bedroom. I tried to distract her but she kept asking questions and worrying about the snake.

'Does Haridada know where the snake's mother stays?'

'The poor snake got lost. It was looking so sad, no, Ma?'

'The snake's mother must be crying at home.'

'Haridada didn't hurt the snake, no?'

I don't want anyone to hurt Omar. Sohini's life is tied up with his. Surely my husband will understand that and not hurt him? I have heard him talking about Muslims at parties and elsewhere. I have asked him why he hates Muslims when our son-in-law is a Muslim. But he is clever and told me not to talk rubbish. He doesn't mean the Omar sort of person when he criticizes Muslims. But I do not believe him. It is like saying he hates our children but not Sohini or Sudeep. Does that make any sense?

I do not know what his exact plan is. He is a man who is angry all the time. He hates me too, but I don't think he will kill me because people might find out. Not that I mind dying at all. I would love to die before I fall ill. All I am doing is sitting and waiting for my life to end in any case. That is how it is after one gets a little old. But Omar has to live. For Sohini and Shazia.

I could help my husband end his life the way I helped his mother before him. That will stop him from being angry with me all the time. And Omar will be safe.

I used to read a lot of Agatha Christies in school. The main poisons used for murder in her novels are arsenic and cyanide. And not just those two; there were so many different chemicals and drugs used to kill people in her books. Agatha Christie had a depth of scientific knowledge that enabled her to do this. I was a good student in school and college and was particularly interested in Chemistry and Maths. If only I had been allowed to study further, I would have had better knowledge of how to administer poison if the situation arose.

I am still pasting news items in the scrapbook that I started sometime ago. I began the project to please my husband, though I might have to use it against him eventually. To show how the world is falling apart, and it is a little bit his fault because he has problems with the things that are happening around us. By talking the way he does he is making the world a bad place. In Delhi there is no *Statesman*, but there are other newspapers. I have been cutting news items about JNU and keeping them in my suitcase. I might have to use them as proof later. I told Sohini but she didn't really understand. Which is a good thing. I don't want her to be involved in all this. It is messy. News in pieces. Chopped up and pasted in my scrapbook.

To take someone's life is not right. We should not try to play God. Gandhi spoke about ahimsa and he was a good man. But Krishna did urge Arjuna to kill in the name of Dharma. There is no point in being too soft and letting evil-doers get away. I have spent my life protecting Sohini from the rest of the family. I must do so till the end. Otherwise it will only be a job half-done.

My life is almost over. I will not be around forever to save my daughter. I need to leave behind a world that doesn't take away all that is important to her. To this end I must work when I get home to my husband. He has been good to me. We have had a good marriage. But all good things must come to an end. And so must this. I have saved all the news I need. I know what is going on in the world now just as my husband wanted me to, and I will now save Omar. Of course I know about almonds and how the bitter ones have the quality of cyanide in them. They can cause dizziness, respiratory troubles, and also death.

Sohini

Ma has gone back to Calcutta and I am consumed by an anxiety, a foreboding, that I can't define.

'Don't worry, I will make sure your Baba doesn't harm Omar in any way,' Ma said on the phone today.

'What?' I asked. I know she has had these thoughts of late. Of Baba as a Hindutva ideologue who wants to decimate Muslims.

'Cutting out the tongue,' she added very lucidly. As ever, I struggled to join the dots. A youth-wing leader of the BJP has announced some prize money for anyone who cuts off the tongue of the JNU Students' Union President, Kanhaiya Kumar. Ma had possibly heard about that or read about it in the papers.

'Those are empty threats being made to students by goons, Ma,' I said.

'I know what is happening in JNU,' she said belligerently as if I was in denial.

'Yes, Ma, but it's all under control,' I said though I didn't really think it was.

'Your father disapproves of it. I am hoping he doesn't want to cut out anyone's tongue, that is all.' Ma sounded cagey, as if she knew something I didn't.

'He doesn't, Ma, of course not,' I said.

'Of course not, of course not,' she echoed as if to mollify me.

Mashi tells me that Ma is much into cooking these days. She is poring over recipe books and putting together meals for Baba. Mashi thinks it is good for her to have a hobby, but it makes me uneasy.

'She has always had these sudden passions, in all fairness,' I say, trying to explain it to myself. 'She used to bake really well. Doughnuts and lemon tarts and pastries.'

'Yes, and she said she is doing a lot of baking.' Mashi sounds optimistic. 'The cook tries to shoo her away but she insists on doing it herself, at least some of it.'

I ask Ma how her cooking is going the next time I speak to her. When she doesn't understand my questions, which happens often, she just says whatever is at the top of her mind. But she gets me this time, though she doesn't ask how I know. Nothing surprises her any more – the brain cell governing surprise has died, I suppose.

'Yes, I am cooking and baking a lot these days, mostly with almonds,' she replies.

'With almonds?' I am amused in spite of myself. Ma is displaying the whimsical randomness of a child once again.

'Almonds in salads, in cakes, in everything,' she says with glee.

'Why almonds?' I ask.

'Why?' she repeats. 'No, no, no reason, nothing. Okay, I have to go.'

While all the thoughts and ideas lodged in her brain slosh around messily, the one thought that has been uppermost since the day I was born refuses to go away. She has to look out for me, keep me safe.

'Omar is in jail,' Ma said today morning on the phone.

'No, Ma, he isn't,' I told her, already feeling tired. I know she has decided for herself and won't change her mind.

'I read it in the newspaper. It is in front of me.'

'Yes, Ma, but it is not Omar. This is Umar Khalid, and sitting next to me here is my husband, Omar. Talk to him.'

I gave Omar the phone. 'Hello Ma.'

He shook his head when he handed the phone back to me. 'At first, she was delighted to hear my voice. Said thank god you are fine, but after two minutes she told me Omar is in jail.'

I rolled my eyes as I put the phone to my ear. She was still talking. 'I don't know what your Baba is up to. But don't worry, I am doing my best. It will be taken care of. After that, I will come and stay with you.'

'That will be good, Ma,' I said.

Ma keeps saying she will take care of 'it'. I have no way to tell what she means. She hints at these conspiracy theories and shuts up if I ask any questions. I don't know if she is unable to process the questions or doesn't wish to answer them.

A week or so later I get a call from Sudeep. Baba has been hospitalized. My father is nearly eighty, but to imagine him in hospital is difficult. By sheer force of will and arrogance he has fought off ill health all these years.

I think of Ma bustling around in the kitchen, bullying the cook, planning each meal for Baba. I don't know if I was expecting what Sudeep says next.

'Food poisoning, from almonds apparently, which sounds strange. I didn't know that was possible.'

Ma is at the airport waiting for me. Next to her is her day nurse, in starched white uniform. The nurse has been there for the last one month or so. I wonder what she thinks of Ma's obsession with cooking. The nurse tells me Baba is doing better.

'Yes, better,' Ma says when we are in the car. She is looking out of the window. 'But very weak, ill, not able to do anything.'

She turns to look at me and there is a slyness in her eyes that I have never seen before. 'Not able to do anything,' she says again.

Ma has dementia, for crying out loud. All of us know that. Her every thought is jumbled. She isn't capable of deliberation and plotting and planning with an aim to harm another person. She really isn't.

Ma is looking at me. 'Is anything the matter? You look worried,' she says. She hasn't asked such a question in a long while. We are now used to her exhibiting the determined selfishness of a two-year-old who doesn't stop to consider others' feelings. Or so I think. So everyone thinks.

'Come back to Delhi with me,' I say impulsively. 'Once Baba is out of hospital.'

'Not so soon,' she replies vaguely. I don't know if she is talking to me or answering some question no one has asked. 'I have things to do. For you. For Omar. After that I will come.'

Soon she will forget about this protecting-Omar bullshit. How long can a dementia patient hold on to a single thought? I will take her away to Delhi for a while. Baba should be left to recover in peace.

'Some things are difficult to forget,' Ma says, as if she has read my mind. I shut my eyes. I will my mind to calm down.

'We are at the hospital, madam,' says the nurse.

Ma is giggling. 'Come, let us go and meet your poor father,' she says.

I want to tell the driver to take us home. I feel drained of all strength. Who is this person who gave birth to me? I will never quite know. Unlike Ma, I don't know whom to protect, whom to save from what. I get out of the car and reluctantly drag myself towards the hospital lobby. Hospital lobbies hold more frayed nerves and collective worries than any other single area in the world. I wonder if I will ever be rid of this feeling. Whether I am going to be stuck forever in the jarring unrest of a hospital lobby.

I look at Ma. She seems frail now. Inconsequential. Her shoulders stoop a little as she shuffles towards the elevator.

She couldn't harm a fly. But then she turns around and looks straight at me. And that sly cagey look is on her face once again. I follow her into the elevator and go up and up to meet my dad. I will my mind to be calm. What am I even thinking? I don't want the elevator ride to end. I don't want Ma and Baba in the same room. But the elevator stops and I follow Ma as she walks towards the room that Baba is in. She remembers the room number and repeats it to me. She remembers. And she has plans. I follow her in. There is not much else I can do.

Acknowledgements

Diya Kar Hazra for saying I should write for adults too and for being my friend, publisher and guide.

Teesta Guha Sarkar for being the sensitive editor that she is and for startling me with so many new thoughts through the last several years since we first met.

Sayoni Basu and Samit Tandon for giving me much critical–loving feedback on the manuscript over tea and cake. And also for insisting I write an Acknowledgements just so I can include their names.

Sankar whose sense of justice and fairness I hope to have imbibed over the years, and Gayathri and Samhitha for being so very silly, smart and funny. And, of course, Rousseau, for stoically accepting that he doesn't have to feature in every book I write.

Nandini Mitra, my mother, for being the most selfless (though she thought she wasn't) and supportive mother ever – and the rest of my family at 7B too.